W9-DDS-113

THE BOBBSEY TWINS
IN THE MYSTERY CAVE

Gradually the hole deepened

The Bobbsey Twins
in the Mystery Cave

By

LAURA LEE HOPE

GROSSET & DUNLAP
Publishers   *New York*

The Bobbsey Twins in the Mystery Cave

CONTENTS

CHAPTER I

FIRE DOG

"RR-RR! Rr-rr!" The Bobbseys' frisky fox terrier raced into the yard where blond, six-year-old Freddie and Flossie were playing badminton with the older twins, dark-haired Bert and Nan. They were twelve.

"Grr-grr!" Waggo repeated, looking up into Freddie's blue eyes, and then darting off again.

"What's the matter with Waggo?" Flossie asked. "He acts 'cited."

"I think he's trying to get Freddie to go some place with him," Bert declared. He grinned. "Maybe he has a cat up a tree!"

Nan tossed her badminton racquet to the ground. "Let's all go," she said. "Perhaps Waggo has found something interesting that he wants to show us."

As she spoke, Waggo bounded down the drive, pausing now and then to look back and bark. The twins hurried after the dog. When Waggo reached the sidewalk, he turned left and ran down the street.

The children followed. Suddenly Bert cried, "He's turning into Susie Larker's drive!" Susie was Flossie's favorite playmate aside from her brothers and sister.

"I see smoke!" Freddie shouted and broke into a run.

When the Bobbseys reached the Larkers' back yard, they saw clouds of black smoke pouring from Susie's playhouse. Susie herself was jumping up and down in excitement.

"I was going to cook my lunch," she wailed, "and the little stove started to smoke, and all the food got on fire! And my bear and my camel will burn up!"

At this moment Mrs. Larker appeared. "Oh dear!" she cried. "I'll call the Fire Department right away." She hurried into the house.

Freddie did not hear her. He was already racing homeward. "I'll get my pumper," he told himself, "and put out that fire! It's lucky Waggo came and got me."

Ever since Freddie had been able to walk, he had played with toy fire engines, and he planned to be a fireman when he grew up. Mr. Bobbsey called him his "little fat fireman."

When Freddie ran into the house he was met by Dinah Johnson, the jolly colored woman who helped Mrs. Bobbsey with the housework. "Now what you up to, Freddie?" she asked suspiciously as she watched him run up the stairs.

"Susie's house is on fire," he called back breathlessly, "and I'm getting my pumper to put it out!"

Dinah threw up her hands. "Don't you go foolin' with any fire, young man!" she cried.

But within half a minute Freddie was out of the house. He ran down the street, dragging his pumper. Hurrying into the Larker yard, he began squirting water furiously into the doorway of the playhouse. By this time Bert had attached the garden hose and was about to send a stream of water through a window.

Nan meanwhile had found a rake and after covering her face with a handkerchief, she fished inside the little building. Out came a smoky-looking toy camel and a Teddy bear.

Freddie's pumper did a good job, and all the smoke died away even before Bert could squirt the hose.

Clang! Clang! A Lakeport fire engine pulled up to the house and three men wearing helmets jumped out. "Where's the fire?" one of them called.

"It's out!" Flossie cried, beaming. "My twin put it out!"

The fireman looked inquiringly at Mrs. Larker. She smiled. "That's right. Freddie Bobbsey put it out."

Freddie's pumper did a good job

The fireman turned to Freddie. "Well now, sonny, you must be a pretty good fireman. This is the first time a little boy has done our job for us!"

Freddie threw out his chest proudly. "I'm going to be a fireman when I grow up," he announced.

The man patted the little boy on the shoulder. "We'll be proud to have you join us," he said. He swung up onto the fire engine, and it started back to the firehouse.

"Oh, Freddie," Susie cried, "you're a real hero! And Nan and Bert, thank you, too."

"And Waggo," Flossie spoke up. "He's a dog hero. He told Freddie about the fire!"

"That's right," Nan agreed. "He should be awarded first prize."

"I'll put a blue ribbon on him when we get home," Flossie decided.

Waggo was very proud and pranced around all evening showing off his ribbon. The older dog Snap, big and white and shaggy, looked on wonderingly and finally with a great sigh went into the kitchen to go to sleep. Later Bert put both dogs out in their kennel in the back yard for the night.

The next morning at breakfast Mr. Bobbsey picked up his copy of the *Lakeport News*. "Well, Freddie," he exclaimed, "you've made the front page of the newspaper!"

Freddie and Flossie slid from their chairs and ran to the side of their tall, handsome father. "Let's see. Let's see," they chorused.

There, in the most prominent spot, was a picture of Freddie and Waggo. Under it the caption read:

LOCAL SIX-YEAR-OLD PUTS OUT
FIRE AFTER DOG'S WARNING.

"Oh, Freddie," Flossie cried, "you're famous!"

Mrs. Bobbsey, a slender, pretty woman with a pleasant smile, asked, "Where did the reporter get your picture, Freddie?"

Just then the telephone rang. Nan went to answer it. The group at the breakfast table could hear Susie Larker's high, excited voice coming over the wire.

After a long conversation Nan returned. "Susie says a reporter came to their house, and she gave him the picture."

All through breakfast the Bobbseys discussed the newspaper article, which also mentioned Nan. Nan picked up the paper and looked at the picture and article. As she turned the other pages she said suddenly, "Here's something interesting!"

"What is it?" Bert asked. "Another fire?"

"No," his twin answered, giggling. "Someone wants to buy a special garnet."

"Let's see it, dear," said Mrs. Bobbsey, holding out her hand for the newspaper. "Oh, it's the Cottrells!" she announced as she began to read. "Richard, you remember Amy and Albert Cottrell. They are lapidaries and own and operate the Rock Shop in Lakeport."

"Lapidary!" Freddie exclaimed. "I thought that was an animal like a camel."

"You're thinking of a dromedary, son," Mr. Bobbsey answered. "A lapidary is a person who cuts and polishes stones like diamonds and garnets."

"Oh," said Freddie.

"Why are the Cottrells looking for a garnet, Mother?" Bert asked.

Mrs. Bobbsey read on. "It seems that they want it for a special order and haven't been able to find the exact kind of stone they want."

"Who do you suppose has ordered it?" Nan wondered dreamily. "Probably a prince!"

"Wa-ait a minute, Nan!" her father teased. "Garnets are only semi-precious stones. I doubt that a prince would be interested. However," Mr. Bobbsey went on, "a hundred years ago Lakeport was noted for its garnets. They were called 'precious' garnets because they were very popular for jewelry. The stones are transparent and deep red in color."

"Aren't there any around here any more?" Bert queried.

"I haven't heard of any stone being found in

this neighborhood recently," his father replied. "They used to turn up once in a while in iron ore at the old iron mines outside of town."

Mr. Bobbsey explained that no mines were being operated at the moment but that the section was still known as Mine Hill.

"Wouldn't it be fun to take a picnic and go out there?" Nan said. "Maybe we could find a garnet for the Cottrells!"

"Oh, yes," Flossie agreed, jumping up and clapping her hands. "May we, Mother?"

Mrs. Bobbsey thought a minute. "Yes, I can take you today. And I guess Dinah can find enough food. Would you like to ask some of your friends to go with us?"

Dinah came into the room at this moment to clear the breakfast table and heard the plans. "I got plenty of fixin's for sandwiches," she volunteered. "And I'm just mixin' up a cake if you want to take that."

Flossie ran over and threw her arms around the smiling cook. "Oh, Dinah," she cried, "you're so good to us! And your cakes are good, too." Dinah chuckled and left the room with the breakfast dishes.

It was decided that each of the twins should invite one friend to join them for the trip to Mine Hill.

"I'll call Charlie," Bert decided. Charlie Mason, a brown-eyed boy with a merry smile, was Bert's classmate in school.

"And I'll ask Nellie Parks," Nan said, starting for the telephone to dial her best friend.

Freddie and Flossie decided to invite their two little playmates, Teddy Blake and Susie Larker. By eleven o'clock the lunch had been packed and stowed in the back of the station wagon, and Mrs. Bobbsey was ready to leave.

"There won't be room in the car for all of us," she said. "Bert, how about you and Charlie riding your bicycles?"

"Okay," Bert agreed. "We'll meet you out there."

"Mother, may Waggo come too?" Flossie pleaded. "He deserves a treat 'cause he was so brave yesterday."

Mrs. Bobbsey smilingly agreed, and Waggo jumped up into the front seat between Nan and Flossie.

The first stop was at the Parks' home. Nellie, a pretty, blond girl, ran out to the car. "Oh, this is fun," she said. "Your idea of a garnet hunt sounds exciting!" She climbed in.

After two more stops to pick up Susie and Teddy, Mrs. Bobbsey drove out to Mine Hill and parked in the shade of a large tree. In a few minutes Bert and Charlie came pedaling up to the others.

"How about a game of ball first?" Bert suggested as he parked his bike next to Charlie's.

The others agreed, and soon a lively game of soft ball was in progress. Suddenly Bert paused just as he was about to throw the ball. "Oh, oh," he muttered, "here comes trouble!"

On the road were two boys on bicycles. One was Danny Rugg, who was Bert's age but heavier and taller. The other was Danny's pal, Jack Westley. Seeing the Bobbseys and their friends, they stopped.

"Hi!" Danny hailed them. "What are you doing out here?"

"We're having a picnic," Teddy Blake explained.

"How about letting us in on it?" Danny asked, looking inquiringly at Mrs. Bobbsey.

As she started to reply, Bert spoke up. "There's always trouble when you're around, Danny," he objected.

"Aw, come on," the boy said, "Jack and I won't hurt your old picnic."

"We'll be glad to have you stay, Danny," Mrs. Bobbsey said, "if you'll play nicely with the other children."

"Oh, sure, Mrs. Bobbsey. We'll be good."

Quickly the picnic lunch was spread out on a white cloth under the tree. Dinah's gleaming chocolate cake was set in one corner.

Danny pulled a glass jar from his pocket. "I have something for you, Flossie. Do you like nuts?"

The little girl took the jar and began to unscrew it. Suddenly a long, green imitation snake leaped out! Flossie screamed and stumbled backward.

The next instant she lost her balance and sat down squarely on the chocolate cake!

CHAPTER II

PICKAX PETE

FOR a moment, after Flossie had fallen into the cake, everyone was too surprised to speak. Then Bert rushed at Danny with clenched fists.

"You big bully, you," he shouted. "I'll teach you to scare my little sister!"

Danny did not wait to hear any more. He and Jack ran to their bicycles, jumped on, and in another second were pedaling furiously down the road.

"The meanie!" Nan cried.

Too often Danny Rugg made things hard for the twins in their adventures. He had not been around to bother them, however, in their latest fun and excitement which had been AT LONDON TOWER in England.

Mrs. Bobbsey and Nan quickly helped Flossie up, and soon had the sticky icing wiped from her dress. The little girl's lips trembled, and there were tears in her eyes as she quavered, "I've spoiled Dinah's bee-oo-ti-ful cake!"

"Never mind, dear," her mother said comfortingly. "You couldn't help it. Danny Rugg is a very mischievous boy!"

The children sat down in a circle around the cloth and were soon munching delicious sandwiches while Mrs. Bobbsey poured cups of milk from two large vacuum bottles.

When they had finished eating, the twins' mother suggested playing a quiet game before starting the search for the mine. "I know one," Nellie said. "Let's play I Pack My Trunk."

"Yes," said Teddy Blake, "I like that game."

Bert explained to Charlie that the first player says, "I am packing my trunk to go to Paris, and I shall put in—" He mentions any article that comes into his head. The game proceeds with each player repeating all the previous articles named and adding one of his own. Whoever makes a mistake is out of the game, and the person who stays in longest is the winner.

"You start, Nellie."

"I'm packing my trunk," Nellie said, "and I shall put in a needle."

"I'm packing my trunk," Nan went on, "and I shall put in a needle and a doll."

The game went on with one player after another having to drop out. Finally Nan and Teddy Blake were the only ones left. Then Nan missed, and Teddy proudly shouted:

"I'm packing my trunk to go to Paris and I'm taking a needle, a doll, a spider, a chocolate cake, a bracelet, a baseball bat, a fireman's hat, a storybook, and a lapidary!"

Everyone applauded, then Nan said, "Where's Waggo? I haven't seen him lately."

"Listen!" said Bert. "I hear him barking. He must be chasing rabbits." He got up and walked a few steps away from the group.

There came an especially sharp yelp and then silence. Flossie jumped up. "Waggo's in trouble! We must find him!"

Quickly the search got underway. The children separated and went in different directions calling the little dog. There was no answering bark.

Then Charlie suddenly shouted from the far side of a little hill. "Come here! I've found something!"

They all ran to join him. Charlie was standing at the entrance to a small shack. The door hung open. Peering in, they could see that the planking which had served as a floor had been pushed aside at one spot, leaving a large hole. But there was no sign of Waggo.

"Oh!" cried Susie Larker. "Do you s'pose he fell down there?"

Bert knelt on the planking and called down the hole, "Here, Waggo! Here, Waggo!"

They all listened intently. Then they heard a little whine. Waggo was down there!

"Mother, how can we ever get him out?" Flossie asked tearfully.

"Don't worry, dear," Mrs. Bobbsey said. "We'll rescue Waggo some way." Turning to Bert, she said, "I think you and Charlie had better get on your bikes and go to the lumberyard. Ask your father or Sam to come out and help us."

Bert and Charlie hurried off while the others settled down to wait. Flossie called down the hole, "Don't cry, Waggo. Help is coming!"

Mr. Bobbsey owned a lumberyard on the shore of Lake Metoka. Sam, Dinah's husband, was his handyman and truck driver. When the boys arrived at the lumber office, Mr. Bobbsey and Sam were checking a newly arrived shipment.

"Why, hello, boys," Bert's father said in surprise. "I thought you had gone to Mine Hill for a picnic."

Bert quickly explained about Waggo's accident. "Please help us get him out."

"Of course," Mr. Bobbsey said briskly. "Sam, put a rope in the truck. This checking can wait."

Sam hurried off. As the twins' father walked toward the truck which was parked nearby, he continued, "You boys had better ride with us. It will be quicker and you can show us exactly where the shack is."

"Okay, Dad. We'll leave our bikes here by the office," Bert agreed.

In a few minutes Sam returned with the rope, and the rescue party started off.

As they drove up Mine Hill, Flossie came running to meet them. "Oh, Daddy, I'm so glad to see you. Waggo is awful scared down in that hole by himself."

"We'll have him out in no time," Mr. Bobbsey assured his small daughter.

"We sure will," Sam agreed, showing his white teeth in a big smile. "Waggo's my friend, and I'm goin' right down there and get him!"

"Wait a minute, Sam," Mr. Bobbsey cautioned. "I think maybe it would be better if one of the boys went. They are smaller and lighter."

"Let me, Dad," Bert pleaded eagerly.

It was agreed that Bert should be the one to go down into the hole. Quickly Sam tied one end of the rope to the axle of the truck and the other under Bert's arms. Then the boy was slowly lowered.

"All right," he called a few moments later. "I have Waggo!"

Inch by inch the rope was raised until Bert came into view. In his arms he held a very subdued Waggo. Freddie reached down and grabbed the little dog, who licked his face gratefully.

Flossie rushed up and threw her arms around the pet. "Waggo, I'm so glad to see you. I thought you were lost forever!"

The terrier ran around, barking happily as if to say, "Thank you for rescuing me!"

"What was down that hole, Bert?" Charlie asked curiously.

"I couldn't see very well," his friend replied, "but it looked like an old mine."

"I think that's just what it is," Mr. Bobbsey said. "There used to be a mine on this hillside. The property is owned by a man named Peterson."

"Did he work the mine?" Bert asked.

Mr. Bobbsey explained that Peterson's father had originally owned the mine. When he gave up mining, his son had taken over. It had never been a large operation and the ore had been taken out with the help of only a few miners.

"Why was the mine closed, Richard?" Mrs. Bobbsey questioned.

Her husband shook his head. "I don't know. Probably it was too small to be operated profitably and Peterson just gave up."

"Does Mr. Peterson still live in Lakeport?" Nan asked.

"Yes, he does. As a matter of fact, a friend of his was in the office just the other day and told me Peterson was living in a small cottage not far from here."

"Maybe we could go to see him and ask if he knows where there are any Lakeport garnets now," Nan suggested.

"He might be very glad to talk to you some time. I imagine he gets lonely there all by himself," Mr. Bobbsey replied. Then he went on, "Right now Sam has to get back to the lumberyard. I'll ride home with you, Mary."

"Charlie and I'll go back with Sam because we have to pick up our bikes," Bert said. "See you all later."

The boys climbed into the truck cab and were soon at the lumberyard. Sam let them off at the office, then drove on into the yard.

As Charlie walked over to the place where the boys had left their bicycles, he said, "I must go home, Bert. See you tomorrow."

"Okay." Bert swung onto his bicycle and prepared to pedal off. But the front wheel wobbled crazily. Looking down, he exclaimed, "Good night! Both tires are flat!"

At the same instant Charlie discovered that the air was out of his tires also. "That's funny," he mused. "Someone must have done this deliberately."

"And I have a good idea who did it," Bert said, hitting his palm with his fist.

"Danny, of course!" his pal agreed.

Bert walked into the office and spoke to his father's clerk. "Did you notice any boys out here where we left our bikes?" he asked.

"Why, yes," the clerk replied. "A dark-haired boy about your age was examining them just a short while ago. Did he do any damage?"

"He let the air out of the tires," Bert replied grimly. "But I have a pump. We'll fix them in a jiffy."

Bert returned to Charlie. "Just as I thought," he said, "Danny! I vote that when we get the tires pumped up, we ride around to Mr. Danny Rugg's house and have a talk with him!"

"Suits me!"

As soon as their task was done the boys rode to Danny's house. When Mrs. Rugg came to the door, she told them that Danny had been away all day.

"He and Jack went out in the country on their bicycles," she explained. "I'll tell him when he gets back that you came to see him."

Bert and Charlie thanked her and left.

That evening the twins talked about the abandoned mine. "Let's go to see Mr. Peterson tomorrow morning and ask him to tell us about it," Nan proposed. The others eagerly agreed.

The next day, after Nan and Flossie had made the beds and Bert and Freddie had swept the walks, they all set off on their bicycles. Mr. Peterson's cottage was not hard to find. It stood in a little grove of trees at the foot of Mine Hill.

At their knock the door was opened by a man about sixty-five years old. He was of medium height, with white hair and a neat beard. His blue eyes twinkled when he smiled.

"Come in!" he greeted them. "I'm glad to have company."

Bert was the spokesman. "We're the Bobbsey twins," he said. "This is my twin, Nan, and the younger ones are Freddie and Flossie."

"I'm glad to meet you," the elderly man replied. "I'm Pickax Peterson. You children just call me Pickax Pete. All my friends do."

They walked into the comfortable living room and sat down. "Mr. Peterson—Pickax Pete—"

Nan began, "we had a picnic near your mine yesterday—"

"Waggo fell in it!" Flossie interrupted.

Pickax Pete was upset to hear this. "Why, I put up a shack to cover the shaft entrance and padlocked the door!"

Nan and Bert explained that the door had been open and the planks pushed aside. Pickax Pete looked very disturbed at hearing this. But in a moment he asked what he could do for his callers.

"Our dad told us that you used to run the mine, and we'd like to hear more about it," Bert explained.

"Well, I'll tell you," Pickax Pete started, crossing his legs and pulling at his beard. "When I was a young 'un I wanted to travel. So I left home and went out West. Out there I got me a job workin' in a gold mine. I'd helped my daddy in his mine here, so I knew a little about minin'."

"Oo, that sounds 'citing," Flossie cried, her blue eyes wide.

"I liked it out West," Pickax Pete went on, "but when my daddy died and left me his mine here, I decided to come back to Lakeport and work it."

"Why did you close your mine, Pickax Pete?" Nan asked.

The old man looked troubled. He shook his

head sadly and said, "My miners wouldn't work it any more because they said the place was haunted!"

CHAPTER III

THE FORTY-NINERS

"HAUNTED!" Bert exclaimed. "Why would they say that?"

"Well." Pickax Pete rubbed his beard again. "There were kind of funny noises around there, and every once in a while a shovel or a pickax would just up and disappear!"

"But there must have been some explanation," Bert insisted.

Pickax Pete shook his head. "None that I could find," he admitted. "Miners are apt to be superstitious critters, and when the word got 'round that there were ghosts down there, they just wouldn't work."

The elderly miner went on to explain that since the mine had never paid very well, he had decided to close it. He had sold all the machinery and covered the shaft with the little shack.

"I don't know as I did the right thing, though," he remarked. "Without a little income from the mine, I'm gettin' sort o' short on money!"

Kind-hearted Nan looked worried. Then suddenly her face brightened. "I have an idea!" she exclaimed.

"What's that, young lady?"

"Why don't you fix the mine up as it used to be and take sightseers through it?"

"Would anybody want to see an old mine?" Pickax Pete asked skeptically.

Bert caught Nan's enthusiasm. "If we're interested, why wouldn't other people be? I think it's a great idea!"

"How did the mine look, Pickax?" Freddie queried.

Pickax Pete explained that the shaft ran down into the ground as far as the mining was carried on. An elevator in the shaft, called a cage, carried the miners up and down to their work. At the foot of the shaft was a room known as the "station."

"This was the office for work being done on that level," Pickax explained. He said that extending from this space were corridors or "galleries" leading to the places where the ore was taken out. These locations were called "stopes."

Then the miner turned to Freddie. "Did you know that there are giraffes and grizzlies in a mine?" he asked, his eyes twinkling.

Freddie looked astonished. "Giraffes and bears down under the ground?" he asked.

"That's right." Pickax chuckled. "The giraffe is a car built to run on inclines. The back wheels are large and the front ones small so the car is always level and will not spill out what's in it."

Flossie giggled. "And what's a grizzly, Mr. Pickax?"

"A grizzly is a screen of horizontal iron bars on which the ore is poured. The dust and small pieces fall through the bars while the good ore stays on top."

"I think I like grizzly bears better," Freddie commented. "I've seen them in the zoo."

By this time Pickax Pete was becoming very much interested in the idea of restoring the mine. He discussed plans with the children until Nan suggested that it was time for them to go home.

"Come again," Pickax said as he went to the door with the twins. "I like your idea and want you to help me carry it out."

They promised to return and rode home. Excitedly the four children told their parents and Dinah and Sam of the morning's adventure and Nan's suggestion of restoring the mine.

"Will you sell Pickax the lumber he needs?" Freddie asked anxiously. "I don't think he has much money."

Mr. Bobbsey smiled. "I'd like to help him. I'll let him have the lumber at exactly the price it costs me."

Flossie ran across the room and threw her

arms around her father. "Oh, you're just the kindest daddy in the world!" she cried as she kissed him.

That afternoon Charlie came over to see Bert, and soon Nellie walked into the back yard where the children were playing. Nan and Bert told them about the visit to Pickax Pete's.

"He's just darling, Nellie," Nan cried, "and we're going to help him restore his mine so he can take sightseers through it!"

"That sounds keen," Charlie said. "Can't we all join you?"

"Sure, that would be great," Bert agreed.

"Yes," said Nan. "I know! We can form a club to help Pickax restore the mine!"

"Right!" cried Nellie. "And we'll call ourselves the Forty-niners after the old miners in the West."

Freddie and Flossie were playing nearby and heard the discussion. "Freddie and I want to be Fort-miners too!" she said, running up to Nan.

"Forty-niners, dear! You and Freddie are a little small, but we'll make you honorary members. They're very important people!"

Flossie looked satisfied. She ran back and whispered to Freddie. Then in a moment she announced, "Freddie and I are going to build a pretend mine shaft."

The little twins ran over to the garage and returned pulling a stepladder. They set it up, then ran back for a wood plank. While the older children watched, Freddie and Flossie propped the plank against the stepladder.

"There's the mine shaft," Flossie explained. "Now we'll fix the cage." She picked up a small fruit basket from the back step and fastened her jumping rope to its handle.

Just at that moment Snoop, the Bobbsey cat, walked by. Flossie, with an impish grin on her face, caught the pet up in her arms. Holding Snoop in the basket while Freddie steadied the stepladder, she climbed to the top.

"Watch!" she cried. "Here goes the elevator!" Grasping the rope, she pushed the basket with the cat down the inclined plank.

But just then Waggo ran around the corner of the house, his tail wagging and his ears pricked up. Snoop saw him coming and with one mighty leap jumped out of the basket and landed in the apple tree! Over went the plank, the ladder, and Flossie!

"Oh, honey, are you hurt?" Nan cried, racing over to her little sister and picking her up.

Tears ran down Flossie's cheeks. "Snoop is a bad miner! And my head hurts!"

Hearing all the commotion, Dinah rushed from the kitchen. "What happened?" she asked. When the cook saw Flossie in tears, she took her from Nan. "You just come with me, honey. Dinah'll fix up that bump with some nice ice!"

Over went the plank, the ladder, and Flossie!

In a few minutes Flossie returned looking cheerful with an adhesive bandage on her head and a cookie in her hand.

"Come on, Flossie," Freddie called. "Where's my cookie?"

"Here are cookies for you all," Dinah announced as she came from the house carrying a plate of luscious-looking ginger cookies.

When Mrs. Bobbsey drove up a little later the Forty-niners were busy making plans for the mine project. Seeing Flossie's bandage, her mother asked, "What happened to you?"

"I had a mining accident," Flossie announced proudly. "The shaft fell down!"

"And Flossie with it!" Nan explained. "But Dinah fixed her up. Mother, would you have time to take us on an errand?" she asked.

"Yes. Where do you want to go?"

"To the Rock Shop so we can meet Mr. and Mrs. Cottrell," Nan replied. "Since they want a garnet so badly, perhaps they'll tell us more about it."

Charlie and Nellie said they could not go as it was time for them to hurry home. But they promised to return for another meeting the next day.

The twins piled into the car, and Mrs. Bobbsey drove to the Cottrells' shop in downtown Lakeport. Amy Cottrell proved to be a small, dark-haired woman with a lively manner and a pleasant smile.

"Mary! How nice to see you!" she cried as the Bobbseys entered the attractive shop.

Mrs. Bobbsey introduced the twins and mentioned their interest in the advertisement for the precious garnet.

"Oh, yes, I'll tell you about that," Mrs. Cottrell said. "But first wouldn't you like to see the shop?"

"I'd like to see a lapidary," Freddie suggested.

Mrs. Cottrell threw back her head and laughed. "You're looking at one, Freddie! Any person who cuts and polishes stones is called a lapidary."

Freddie looked impressed.

"My husband and I are also known as 'rock hounds,'" she said teasingly.

The children all wanted to know what this meant. Mrs. Cottrell explained that people who collected minerals and rocks were known by this name. "It is a very interesting hobby," she went on, "and there are clubs of rock hounds all over the United States."

"Do they meet in kennels?" Bert asked jokingly.

Mrs. Cottrell laughed and led the children around the shop. Arranged along one wall were trays of rock samples, each one labeled with its name and the place where it had been found. On the opposite wall was a glass case filled with attractive handmade jewelry set with semi-precious stones.

Nan exclaimed, "Oh, how lovely!"

"Do you like it?" the shop owner asked. "We make all our own jewelry. I design it, and my husband does the cutting and polishing and setting."

"It's all beautiful, Amy," Mrs. Bobbsey remarked.

Bert was poring over the rock specimens. He had decided that it would be fun to form a club of rock hounds at school.

But Nan was still curious about the garnet. "Won't you tell us, Mrs. Cottrell," she asked, "who ordered the garnet? I'm sure it must be someone very important."

"The person is important to my husband and me," Amy Cottrell replied. "We want it for our daughter's graduation."

Seeing the interested looks on the Bobbseys' faces, she went on, "You see, my grandmother was born in Lakeport and lived here all her life. When she died she left me a very beautiful earring set with a Lakeport garnet."

"Only one earring?" Nan asked.

"Yes. The other one had been lost in her youth. Mr. Cottrell and I thought it would be wonderful if we could make a matching earring for our daughter. But there are not many Lakeport garnets around any more, and we haven't been able to find one of the same deep red color."

"Oh, I do hope you'll find it!" Nan said earnestly. "May we see the old earring?"

"Yes, of course," Mrs. Cottrell replied. "It's right here." She opened a drawer under the glass case. "Why," she cried out, "it's gone!"

CHAPTER IV

A CAKE EXPLOSION

THE antique earring was missing! The Bobbseys looked at one another in dismay.

"Oh! Do you s'pose a robber took it?" Flossie cried, her eyes filling with tears.

Mrs. Cottrell sank into a chair. "I can't believe it's gone," she wailed. "It must be here somewhere." She rummaged furiously through the drawer, but the earring was not there.

"May we help you hunt for it?" Nan asked kindly. "Perhaps you put it some place else."

"Yes. Do look around," Mrs. Cottrell replied. "I was examining it earlier this afternoon when a customer came in. I might have got it mixed up with the other jewelry."

Bert turned back to the display of rock samples. He looked at them carefully. The missing earring was not among them.

On a table nearby was a large tray filled with

unset, semi-precious stones. Nan searched through them, pushing the colored gems aside one by one. "Perhaps the customer was interested in these," Nan said to herself, "and Mrs. Cottrell dropped the earring in here by mistake."

"Have you found it, Nan?" Flossie asked anxiously, coming over to stand by her sister.

"No, I haven't, but we'll keep on looking. Help me sort through these stones."

While Flossie and Nan were bent over the tray of polished gems, Freddie wandered to the back of the shop. Here was a workbench covered with small tools, polishing wheels, and odd settings for jewelry. Far to the back something sparkled.

"I've found it!" Freddie called in excitement. "Here it is!"

Mrs. Cottrell ran to him, smiling happily. Then her expression changed. "Oh, Freddie!" she exclaimed. "I'm afraid that's only a bit of quartz I was cutting for a ring!"

The Bobbseys stood around, feeling as gloomy as Mrs. Cottrell. At that moment the front door opened and a tall, slender man with sandy hair came in. "Albert!" Amy Cottrell called, "I'm so glad you've come!"

Mr. Cottrell hurried over to his wife. "What's the matter? You look pale!"

"The earring is gone!"

"Oh, is that all!" A look of relief spread over Mr. Cottrell's face, and he laughed. "I'm sorry, dear," he said. "I forgot to tell you. I have it. I took the earring over to another rock hound in town. I hoped he might have a garnet to match this one. But no luck!"

"Thank goodness, it hasn't been stolen!" Mrs. Cottrell sighed. "I still think we'll be able to find a matching stone some place."

The Bobbseys admired the heirloom earring, then said good-by. "Come again," the shop owner urged, thanking them for helping with the search. "Nan, if you'd be interested, I'll be happy to show you how to work with stones."

"Oh, I'd love it," Nan replied eagerly. "I'll come back just as soon as I can!"

The next day, since the Forty-niners had agreed to visit Pickax Pete, Nan decided to bake a cake to take to him. Right after breakfast she went into the kitchen and told Dinah her plan.

"That's fine, honey," the cook said. "You make right good old-fashioned cake. I got to be in the basement doin' the laundry, but you just call me if you need anything."

Flossie had followed her sister from the dining room and now spoke up. "I'll help you, Nan. Let me bring all the 'gredients, and you can put them together!"

"All right," Nan agreed, tying aprons first around Flossie, then herself. "We'll begin with butter and sugar, then we'll need milk and eggs."

Flossie obediently trotted to the refrigerator and returned with butter, milk, and eggs. After Nan had mixed the dry ingredients together, she began to combine the butter and sugar. At that moment the telephone rang, and in a few seconds Mrs. Bobbsey called from upstairs, "Nan! Nellie is on the phone and wants to talk to you."

Nan laid down her spoon and hurried from the kitchen. When she did not return at once Flossie grew restless.

"Now what can I do?" she asked herself. Then her eyes lighted up. "I know! I'll help Nan with the cake some more. I didn't see her put in any baking powder, and I know that goes in a cake."

She picked up the can from the table. "I'll put plenty in," she thought, "so the cake'll be nice and high." Carefully, she measured out three tablespoonfuls.

Nan came back into the room. "Nellie and Charlie are coming over right after lunch," she explained, "so I'll hurry up and finish this cake."

In a few minutes the batter was mixed, and Nan popped the two cake pans into the oven. She and Flossie went out into the yard to feed Waggo and Snap and Snoop and wait for the cake to bake.

Some time later Nan went in to look at her cake. She opened the oven door. "Oh, Dinah!" she cried. "Something terrible has happened!"

Dinah ran up the basement stairs as fast as she could and arrived panting. "Wh-what's the matter? Did you burn yourself?"

"No! But look!" Nan wailed, pointing to the oven.

Batter covered the inside and dripped out onto the floor. Dinah threw up her hands in amazement. "Heavens, honey, what did you put in that cake?"

Flossie had run into the kitchen and stopped short at the sight. Suddenly her face grew pink, and tears came into her eyes. "I-I guess it's my fault! I only wanted to make the cake nice and tall," she quavered.

"What do you mean?" Nan asked.

"I—I put in some baking powder," Flossie explained. "I thought you always did!"

Nan smiled in spite of her dismay. "So that's it! Very thoughtful of you, Flossie, except that I had already put in the baking powder."

"Oh, Nan, I'm so sorry!" the little girl cried. "I'll clean up all the mess myself."

Dinah and Nan helped her, and soon the oven and floor were spotless again. Dinah urged the girls to go into the back yard and play.

"Don't you fret about that old cake. I'm about to make some sugar cookies, and there'll be plenty o' them for you to take to that Mr. Pickax." She grinned. "That's a funny name if I ever heard one!"

Nan giggled. "Thank you, Dinah. You're a true friend."

After lunch the Forty-niners gathered in the Bobbseys' yard with their bicycles. Bert carried a large package of the sugar cookies in the wire basket on his bicycle.

It did not take the children long to reach Pickax's little cottage. He came to the door and cried jovially, "Come in! I'm glad to see you all."

Nan introduced Nellie and Charlie and handed him the cookies. He thanked her and then led the children into the living room.

Freddie could hardly wait to tell their news. "Pickax," he said excitedly, "our daddy says he will let you have the lumber you need for your mine at just what he pays for it!"

The elderly man looked pleased. "Well, that's mighty nice of Mr. Bobbsey," he said. "I sure appreciate that!"

Bert explained about the Forty-niners club, and Pickax said he was very flattered and proud to have so many helpers. "I've been studyin' about opening the place to sightseers and I've come up with a few ideas."

"We'd like to hear them," Charlie Mason spoke up.

"Well, in the first place," the old miner went on, "I figger it'd cost too much to put another elevator in the shaft. I sold all the machinery when I closed the mine, and I can't afford to buy new." He paused, then went on, "Now my idea is to build a wooden stairway down to the first level, then fix up the station with a wooden floor, walls, and ceiling."

"The station is the office," Freddie explained importantly to Charlie and Nellie.

Pickax continued. "Then I'll fix up two of the galleries going in opposite directions. The tracks are still there so we can run the giraffe."

"That's a car with funny wheels," Flossie told Charlie and Nellie, not wanting Freddie to appear to know more about mines than she did.

"It sounds keen, Pickax," Charlie said. "I'll bet you'll have lots of sightseers."

Freddie had been thinking. Now he spoke up. "Can't we put some make-believe miners around to scare people?" he suggested.

The others laughed and agreed that it would be a good idea to have figures to look as if they were at work.

Bert had been quiet for some time. "I've been wondering," he said, "about that so-called haunting. It sounds very mysterious to me."

"I never understood it myself," Pickax said.

"Did you ever find anything in that mine except iron? I mean something that would be more valuable?"

"Well, I found a piece of ore one time that had a big garnet in it."

"A garnet!" Nan exclaimed. "We're very interested in garnets."

"Garnets are only semi-precious gems," Pickax explained. "But this particular one was a good, deep red color—a regular old-time Lakeport garnet."

"Do garnets have any other value except for jewelry?" Bert wanted to know.

Pickax explained that they were sometimes used in watch-making and also in powdered form to polish other gems.

"Then it would be worthwhile for a person to find a lot of garnets?" Bert persisted.

Pickax nodded. "Yes, it might give him a nice, steady little income."

Flossie had been impatiently waiting for this conversation to end. Now she said, "Please, Mr. Pickax, may we see your big garnet?"

"I would like to show it to you, little lady, but I don't have it just now. A miner friend of mine, Ben Mullin, borrowed it from me. He's a real rock hound and wanted to show it at his club."

"Where does Mr. Mullin live?" Nellie asked.

"Over in Beechcroft Hill."

"We know where that is," Nan exclaimed.

Nan told Pickax about the ad which the Cottrells had run in the *Lakeport News* and the fact that they were trying to find a real Lakeport garnet to match the one in the antique earring.

"Perhaps yours would be just right for them!" she said excitedly.

"Well now, I'd be glad to sell the garnet if it's

what your friends want. When Ben Mullin returns it, I'll let you know," Pickax said.

"But Pickax," Flossie protested, "Mr. Rock House Cottrell wants it right away! He has to make an earring for his daughter for her graduation."

Pickax shook his head uncertainly. "I don't see what I can do about it now."

"Beechcroft Hill is only about fifteen or twenty miles from here," Nan said. "Perhaps Mother would drive us over there, and we could ask Mr. Mullin for your garnet."

"That's a great idea, Nan!" Bert cried. "We'll ask her when we get home. I'm sure she'll take us!"

"That's mighty nice of you," Pickax said. "You could explain about the Cottrells better than I could. I'm sure when Ben hears about it, he'll be glad to let you bring the garnet back."

"Don't you worry," Flossie said, "we'll get it for you."

The children got up to go. As Nellie walked toward the door, she suddenly screamed and pointed to the front window. "Look! Bert! Nan! Charlie!"

They turned quickly just in time to see two frightening faces, topped by old hats, disappear from the open space!

CHAPTER V

A STRANGE SALESMAN

AS THE heads dropped out of sight, Bert dashed for the door. The other children quickly followed. But they were too late. All they could see were two figures disappearing into the woods.

"Who do you think they were?" Nellie asked, her voice still shaky.

"Danny Rugg and Jack Westley making faces at us!" Flossie said decidedly.

"I don't think so," Bert objected. "I have an idea they were grown-up men from the way they ran."

"That's right," Charlie agreed. "Besides, one was tall and the other much shorter. There isn't that much difference in Danny's and Jack's height."

Realizing that they could not hope to find the men, the children climbed onto their bicycles, waved good-by to Pickax, and rode home. On the way they discussed the trip to Beechcroft Hill. The Bobbseys learned that both Nellie and Charlie were going away with their parents for a few days.

"If your mother can take you tomorrow," Nellie said, "I think you should go. The sooner the Cottrells get the garnet they want, the better."

Charlie agreed with Nellie, so it was decided that the Bobbseys would visit Ben Mullin alone, provided their mother would be able to take them.

When the twins reached home, Nan told her the situation and asked, "Would you drive us to Beechcroft Hill tomorrow?"

"I'll be glad to."

But the twins awoke the next morning to find a pouring rain which continued through the weekend. It was not until the following Tuesday that they were able to make the trip. They started out soon after breakfast and, following Pickax's directions, drove up a short time later to the small brick house where Ben Mullin lived.

In response to their ring, the door was opened by a slender man of medium height with iron gray hair. Mrs. Bobbsey introduced herself and the children.

"Come in," Ben Mullin invited them and led the way into the living room.

The children looked around and saw several cabinets filled with pieces of rocks and minerals.

"Are you a rock dog, Mr. Mullin?" Flossie asked, looking up into the man's face.

Ben Mullin smiled. "I guess you mean rock *hound*. That's what they usually call us rock collectors," he said. "Yes, I'm a member of our local club. What can I do for you?"

"We're friends of Pickax Pete," Nan began. "He says he lent you a piece of ore with a big garnet in it."

"And we'd like to take it back to him," Freddie piped up.

"We-ell, yes." Mr. Mullin looked uneasy. "Just why do you want the garnet today?" he asked.

The twins took turns explaining about the Cottrells and their search for a garnet to match the antique earring. Flossie ended up triumphantly, "So Pickax is going to sell his garnet to them!"

An embarrassed expression came over Mr. Mullin's face. "You see, I haven't got the garnet!" he said desperately.

"Where is it?" Bert asked in surprise.

"I lost it!"

At the children's exclamations, Ben Mullin held up his hand. "Wait a minute! I'll tell you just how it happened."

He explained that the day he had gone to Pickax Pete's house, he had left his car at a garage to be serviced and walked out to Mine Hill.

He had visited awhile with Pickax and then had left, carrying the garnet ore.

"When I came out of the house I noticed Henry Zimmer coming up the road toward me. I didn't want to meet him, so I decided to cut across the hill and go back to town that way."

Flossie broke in, "Who is Henry Zimmer? Don't you like him?"

"I don't trust him. He used to work with me in Pickax's mine. He was always a shifty sort of fellow, and I'm sure he was the cause of a couple of accidents."

"Do go on with your story, Mr. Mullin," Mrs. Bobbsey urged. "Flossie, please don't interrupt again."

"I'm sorry, Mommy."

"Well, as I said, I started up the hill. I'd almost reached the top when I turned around to see if Zimmer was following me. He was! As I tried to climb faster, I stumbled, and that hunk of ore flew right out of my hand and rolled down the hill!"

"Did Mr. Zimmer get it?" Bert asked, his eyes wide.

"I don't know. I ran down as fast as I could and looked for the garnet, but it had completely disappeared. I met Zimmer and asked him if he had seen it. But he said no and hurried away. I searched that entire hillside but never found the garnet."

"Oh, that's terrible, Mr. Mullin!" Nan exclaimed sympathetically.

Ben Mullin said that he had not told Pickax Pete of his loss because he still hoped to find the piece of ore. "If Zimmer didn't pick it up, the garnet must be on that hillside. It couldn't just disappear!"

"We'll help you look for it," Nan volunteered.

"Yes," Freddie agreed enthusiastically. "We Bobbseys are good at finding things—especially mysterious ones!"

"It sure sounds as if Henry Zimmer had picked up that garnet and gone off with it," Bert remarked. "What does he look like, Mr. Mullin?"

"Short, on the stocky side, and bald," the ex-miner replied.

Mrs. Bobbsey expressed her sympathy too, then stood up and said they must start now for Lakeport. As Ben Mullin bade them good-by, he said, "I'd appreciate it if you would explain about the garnet to Pickax. Tell him I'm trying to find it for him."

"We'll do that," Bert assured the man.

He opened the door for his mother. On the porch stood a tall, thin man with untidy black hair! Instantly Bert wondered if he had been listening to Mullin's story.

"You wish to see Mr. Mullin?" Bert asked.

The man looked startled and very nervous.

"Why—uh—no—yes. I—I'm selling books." He held up a worn-looking leather bag.

"What kind of books? Let's see them," the boy insisted.

"I don't th-think you'd like them," the caller stuttered, backing away.

He stumbled, and his arms flailed wildly as he tried to get his balance. The bag flew open. It was empty! And from the man's pocket dropped a piece of ore with what looked like a garnet in it!

Instantly Bert thought, "The lost stone!"

The fellow picked up the bag and the piece of ore, turned and fled. Bert was sure now the man had not come there to return the stone. He rushed after the stranger. But with a head start and longer legs than Bert, the man drew ahead steadily.

Flossie jumped up and down on the porch, squealing, "Catch him, Bert! Catch him!"

The stranger dashed along the street. Old ladies and children quickly got out of his way, then turned to stare questioningly after him. Bert, in pursuit, dodged around a woman pushing a baby carriage, then nearly fell over a little boy pulling a red wagon.

"Watch where you're going, young man!" the boy's mother said tartly.

"I'm very sorry," Bert apologized.

By this time the man was far ahead, but Bert could see him in the next block walking briskly along. The fugitive paused, looked behind him, then turned into a store.

"It's that sporting goods shop with the neon sign," Bert told himself as he increased his speed.

Fortunately the traffic light was green at the intersection and the boy did not slacken his pace. Reaching the sporting goods store, he dashed inside. A customer was just leaving, Bert swerved to avoid him. *Crash!* A piled-up display of cans of tennis balls fell to the floor with a clatter!

The proprietor advanced toward him. "What's the meaning of this?" he asked. "I can't have people running wild through my store!"

Bert glanced around. The tall, thin man was not there. "I beg your pardon, sir," the boy stammered. "I was chasing a man who said he was a book salesman. I thought he came in here."

"Was he tall and thin with a lot of black hair?" the store owner asked.

"Yes," Bert replied eagerly. "Did you see him?"

"He walked right through here and out the back door. He was going pretty fast!"

Bert ran to the back door and looked up and down the passageway behind the store. There was no one in sight.

"I guess I've lost him." He sighed, and helped the proprietor pick up the tennis balls. Then he returned to Ben Mullin's house.

"Did you catch him, Bert?" asked Nan anxiously as her twin came up the walk.

Bert shook his head.

"Who was he?" Freddie inquired.

"I don't know. But he acted funny and when that bag came open and there were no books inside and the ore with the garnet in it fell out of his pocket, I was sure he was a phony. I think he was spying on us!"

Ben Mullin was upset by the whole affair. Who was the stranger, and what did he want? And did he have the lost garnet?

Mrs. Bobbsey spoke up. "There's nothing we can do now. But we'll keep our eyes open for the man. And I suggest, Mr. Mullin, that if you hear from him again, you be very careful."

"And please let us know," Bert begged.

"Yes," Freddie added. "The Forty-niners will come here and protect you!"

The other Bobbseys laughed and Mr. Mullin wanted to know who the Forty-niners were. "It's a secret," Nan said quickly before her small sister could give away the plans for Pickax's mine. "You know, kind of a children's secret club."

"I see," said Mr. Mullin and did not inquire further.

On the way home Flossie sat next to Nan. She took her hand and said, "I didn't know I belonged to a secret club. I won't tell *anybody* about the Forty-niners."

"Not until Pickax makes his announcement about opening the mine to sightseers," Nan said.

Flossie sighed. "Oh dear! We have *so* much to do before that."

"We sure have," Bert agreed. "New shoring, steps, figures—"

"What kind of figures shall we have?" Nan asked. "Wax, wood, plastic?"

Mrs. Bobbsey laughed. "I think you'll take what you can get."

At this moment the car was passing an attractive-looking wayside restaurant. Freddie cried out, "I'm hungry!"

"And I'm thirsty!" Bert joined in.

Mrs. Bobbsey smiled and slowed the car. "How about you, Nan and Flossie? Would you like to stop here for lunch?"

"Oh, yes!"

Soon the five Bobbseys were seated at a table in the cool lunchroom. As they ate sandwiches and drank milk they discussed the loss of Pickax's garnet.

"We must find it," Nan said hopefully. "The Cottrells need the stone, and Pickax needs the money it would bring."

A little later, as the Bobbseys were leaving the restaurant, Bert pulled Nan aside. "I don't want to seem gloomy," he told her, "but I'm sure Zimmer stole that garnet on the hill."

"Maybe not. Anyway, let's not tell Pickax that. We'll just say we'll do our best to find it."

When they arrived at the miner's cottage he

was waiting for them. "Did you bring the garnet?" he asked eagerly.

But his face fell after Bert and Nan told him Ben Mullin's story. "That's too bad," he said. "I'd trust Ben any time. I know he's telling the truth. But I'm sure sorry to lose that garnet."

"We're sorry too, Mr. Peterson," Mrs. Bobbsey consoled him. "But maybe the twins can locate it for you."

The old miner shook his head. "This is my bad luck day, I guess. Somethin' else happened this morning."

"What was that, Pickax?" Bert asked.

"Henry Zimmer was here. He offered to buy my mine!"

CHAPTER VI

THE RESCUE CAGE

"BUY your mine!" Nan repeated. "Why should he want to do that?"

Pickax Pete shrugged. "I don't know, but I've half a mind to sell. The trouble is, he didn't offer much money for it."

"Oh, you mustn't sell to him, Pickax," Nan exclaimed. "I'm sure you can make more money by taking sightseers through it. We'll help fix it up, and all our friends will come to see the mine."

Bert spoke up too. "I wouldn't trust that Zimmer. Perhaps he stole the piece of ore on the hill and wants to buy the mine because he thinks he can find more garnets in it!"

"Of course, that could be," Pickax agreed, "but he'd be fooled. I don't think there's much garnet in that mine."

"Please don't sell the mine, Mr. Pickax," Flossie pleaded. "Freddie and I want to be miners."

Pickax laughed and ruffled Flossie's blond curls. "I won't sell for a while anyway. We'll find out how the sightseeing turns out."

"How is the work coming along?" Bert queried.

"Just fine. When are you Bobbseys coming out to look at what's been done?"

"May we look right now?" Freddie asked excitedly.

Mrs. Bobbsey glanced at her watch. "Not right now," she said. "I have an engagement and must get home. But you children may get your bicycles and meet Pickax at the mine later if you want to."

Flossie clapped her hands. "Goody! We'll see you, Mr. Pickax."

When they arrived home Flossie hurried upstairs to her bedroom.

After waiting for her a few minutes, Nan called, "Come on, Flossie! We're ready."

"Just a minute. I'm getting the children dressed!" the little girl replied.

She came down carrying her two favorite dolls. "Linda and Marie want to see the mine, too," she explained. "They can ride in Bert's bicycle basket. "

Bert objected. "I'd look awfully silly riding along with a couple of dolls!" he said disgustedly.

"You can put a sign on them saying, 'These

are my sister's dolls,'" Nan teased him.

Her brother grinned. "Okay, Floss, I'll take them. All I hope is that we don't meet Danny Rugg! He'd kid me the rest of my life!"

Flossie settled the dolls in the basket and stood back to admire them.

"You look just lovely," she cried. "Don't be afraid. Bert will take care of you!"

"Let's make this snappy," Bert urged, swinging onto his bicycle and pedaling rapidly down the driveway.

Nan and the little twins followed, and the procession turned toward Mine Hill. They rode along in silence for a few minutes until they reached an intersection and had to stop for a traffic light.

"Oh!" Bert groaned. "Look across the street!"

There, waiting for the signal to change, were Danny and Jack on their bicycles. When the light turned green Bert pedaled rapidly across, hoping to escape Danny's notice.

But he heard a shout, "Hey! Look at that!"

Danny quickly made a U-turn and drew up beside Bert.

"Ha, ha," he jeered. "Bert Bobbsey plays with dolls!"

Bert pedaled faster, trying to ignore the bully's taunts. But by this time Jack had joined his friend.

"Are you taking the babies for a ride?" Jack asked in a high, girlish voice.

"You let my brother alone!" Nan spoke up.

"Don't pay any attention to them, Nan," Bert advised, riding as fast as he could. "They just think they're smart!" But his face was red.

"And where are you taking the children?" Danny persisted, using the same high-pitched voice that Jack had.

"We're taking them to our mine, Danny Rugg!" Flossie spoke up.

"Oh, you have a mine?" Danny asked, pretending to be impressed.

"Yes, and we're going to fix it all up," Freddie added proudly.

"You're a bunch of silly kids!" Danny scoffed. As he rode off, he called back, "By-by, Bert the baby sitter!"

"By-by, Dan, you great big quitter!" Freddie retorted.

Flossie giggled at her little brother, and Nan and Bert laughed as they went on their way.

"I'm not sure it was a good idea to tell Danny about the mine," Nan remarked as they rode along.

"Why not, Nan?" Flossie asked.

"Well, you know Danny," her sister replied. "If he knows what we're doing, he may try to make trouble."

When the twins reached Mine Hill they found Pickax Pete already there. Proudly he showed them the new shack which had been built over the shaft.

"Why, Pickax!" Nan exclaimed in amazement. "How did you do all this in such a short time?"

Pickax looked pleased. "One of my old buddies, Jim Borden, helped me. Jim's a pretty good carpenter."

The shaft opening was about five feet square. From it the stairs descended.

"The steps are in down to the first level," Pickax Pete told the children. "We've finished them and the station at the bottom. I'll take you down."

He reached up and rang a little bell which hung from the ceiling.

"What's that for?" Freddie asked.

"Well, you see, whenever a miner's cage starts down the shaft a bell is rung. The same thing happens when the cage comes up again. Even though our 'cage' is a stairway, I thought we ought to carry out the old idea."

"Is anybody down there to hear the bell?" Nan asked.

"Oh, yes. Jim's working on the station. This will let him know that we're comin'."

Pickax led the way down the long flight of stairs. It grew cooler and darker the farther they went. Then they saw a glimmer of light below.

"I have some electric lanterns spotted around so we can see," the old miner explained.

At the foot of the stairs the group stepped into a room which had been freshly walled, roofed and floored with wooden planks. Out from it at opposite sides ran two dark corridors. The children could dimly see car tracks vanishing into the gloom.

"Those are the galleries, aren't they, Pickax?" Nan asked, remembering what the elderly man had told them when he was describing the mine.

"That's right. And tomorrow I'll have the giraffe up to the station."

Freddie giggled. It still seemed funny to him that a car which ran on tracks should have an animal's name.

At this moment a man in overalls emerged from one of the corridors. Pickax introduced him as Jim Borden. The man was tall and thin with gray hair and a pleasant, weather-beaten face.

"It's a good idea you children had, to restore this mine," he said. "We're getting the galleries fixed up now."

"We think you've done a fine job," Bert complimented him.

"It's too bad we can't have a real elevator in the shaft." Flossie sighed as she looked upward. "Freddie and I could run it."

"And take the miners up and down," her twin agreed. Then his face brightened. "We *could* have a cage anyway!" he said.

"How?"

Freddie ran over and whispered in Pickax's ear. The miner smiled and nodded.

"You wait here a minute," Freddie instructed. Then he and Pickax went back up the steps.

"What do you suppose they're up to?" Bert asked uneasily.

When Pickax Pete and Freddie reached the top of the shaft again, the little boy ran over to Bert's bicycle.

"See! This is what I mean," he explained to the old miner. "Have you some string?"

As Pickax rummaged through his pockets, Freddie unfastened the wire basket from Bert's bicycle. The dolls, Linda and Marie, were still in it.

Pickax produced a ball of twine. Together they tied the string to the basket, then went back into the shack. While Pickax rang the little bell, Freddie leaned over the stairway and began to lower the basket with the dolls in it.

From below he could hear Flossie's delighted giggle as she spied Linda and Marie coming down the shaft. Then *snap!* the twine broke, and the basket-elevator fell to the bottom!

"Oh!" Flossie wailed. "My poor dolls! Linda and Marie will be killed!"

"Oh! My poor dolls!" Flossie wailed

Pickax acted quickly. "Flossie!" he called down the shaft. "You and Bert and Nan come on up. We'll have a mine rescue!"

In a few seconds Flossie's blond curls appeared at the top of the shaft. Her face was tear-streaked. Bert and Nan were behind her.

"Now, Flossie," Pickax instructed, "you stand right here. Freddie and I will show you how miners are brought out when there is an accident "

He handed Freddie the ball of twine. "When I ring the bell down below, you let out a little more string," he explained. "And when I ring the second time you start pulling."

With that, the miner rang the signal bell and hurried down the steps. A few seconds later the bell tinkled. Carefully Freddie unwound some string and let it dangle into the open shaft.

Then the watchers saw the twine grow taut. The bell rang again, and Freddie began to pull the string.

"Here they come!" Flossie cried excitedly as the basket with the dolls began to move slowly up the shaft. "Oh, I hope they won't fall!"

But this time Pickax Pete climbed the stairs at the same rate of speed, holding onto the rescue cage.

When the basket reached the top and the miner stepped out onto the floor of the shack, Flossie rushed over and picked up her dolls.

"Oh, you poor children!" she exclaimed. "What a terrible 'sperience you've had!" She examined them carefully, then said in relief, "But you're hardly hurt at all!"

As the others watched, Flossie ran outside. In a second she returned, her hands behind her back. She ran up to Pickax and asked him to stoop down.

"I want to give you a life-saving medal!" she announced.

CHAPTER VII

THE DEEP HOLE

"THERE!" said Flossie, smiling at Pickax Pete. She stuck a dandelion in the buttonhole of his jacket.

Pickax grinned and thanked Flossie for his medal, saying he hoped Linda and Marie would soon recover from their fall.

"I think they'll be fine after a good night's sleep," Flossie replied solemnly, but with a twinkle in her blue eyes.

Nan suggested that the twins start for home. "Thank you, Pickax, for showing us the mine. You'll soon be ready for the opening, won't you?" she said.

"I hope so," the miner replied.

"Good-by, Mr. Pickax," Flossie called as the children mounted their wheels for the ride to Lakeport. "We'll be back soon."

The following day Charlie and Nellie both telephoned to say that they had returned, and it was decided to have a meeting of the Forty-niners at once. When they all gathered at the Bobbsey home, Nan and Bert gave Charlie and Nellie a complete account of their visit to Ben Mullin.

"Who do you suppose that strange man was, Bert?" Nellie asked. "It's too bad he got away!"

"It sure was, but I have a feeling we may see him again."

"So Ben Mullin lost the garnet," Charlie mused. "Perhaps we can find it for him."

"That's what we thought," Nan agreed.

"Let's go out to Mine Hill now and look!" Nellie suggested enthusiastically.

"Good idea," the others chorused.

Freddie and Flossie insisted upon going, and soon the six children were pedaling toward Pickax's property.

"Let's divide into two teams for our hunt," Bert proposed. "In that way we should be able to cover every bit of the hill."

The children parked their bicycles at the bottom. Bert, Nellie, and Flossie went to look over the near side of the hill, while Charlie, Nan, and Freddie took the far side. For a while there was silence as the teams spread out and walked slowly up the slope.

The hill was covered with small trees and low bushes with frequent outcroppings of rock. The children searched carefully under all the bushes, pushing aside the low branches and examining the ground underneath. They circled every rock and looked on all sides.

Suddenly Charlie called out, "I've found something!"

The others ran to where Charlie was kneeling on the ground. He was bent over, peering into a little hole.

"I see something bright down here," he said. "Hand me a stick, somebody."

Bert ran to a nearby bush and broke off a low branch. He quickly pulled off the leaves and put the stick into Charlie's outstretched hand. The boy poked the branch down the hole. There was a little flurry in the ground and a few yards away a woodchuck ran out of another hole. It scurried down the hill and under a pile of dead leaves!

"Ha! A live garnet!" Bert hooted.

Nellie laughed. "A woodchuck with garnet eyes!"

Charlie took the teasing good-naturedly. "I'd like to see one of you find something better!" he retorted.

"Well, Charlie, if you find any more garnets running around, let us know," Bert needled his chum.

The group spread out again, but by this time Freddie and Flossie had tired of the search.

"Let's have a race rolling down the hill," Freddie suggested to his twin.

Flossie readily agreed, and the little twins looked around until they found a smooth area which stretched to the bottom of the hill with no trees, rocks, or bushes to stop them.

The twins threw themselves on the grass, and in a moment both were rolling over and over, faster and faster until they arrived breathless at the foot of the slope.

"I won!" Freddie announced as he picked himself up.

"Why, Freddie Bobbsey," his sister exclaimed indignantly, "how can you say that? I was way ahead of you!"

Freddie shrugged and trudged up the hill, whistling as he went. When he reached the top the little boy pulled a ball from his pocket and began tossing it into the air. Flossie watched him.

Freddie continued throwing the ball, then running forward to catch it. Suddenly he stumbled and missed. The ball rolled part way down the hill, then disappeared!

"Oh, you've lost it!" exclaimed Flossie, who had tried to catch the ball before it got away.

"That's all right," said Freddie. "I watched where the ball went. It's right by that stone."

They ran to the big boulder, but the ball was not there. "That's funny," Freddie said.

Both children looked around but could not find the ball. Then Freddie noticed a hole under one side of the stone. "I guess my ball rolled down there," he decided. "I'll get it out."

The little boy lay full length on the ground and stretched his arm down the hole. He could not feel the bottom.

"Bert!" he called to his brother, who had paused in the shade of a tree to rest.

"What is it?"

"I've lost my ball. Please get it for me."

Bert strolled over to where Freddie lay sprawled on the ground. "Where did you lose it?"

"I think it went in this hole," the little boy replied, "but I can't reach it."

Bert lay on the ground and stretched his arm down the hole. "Say, I can't reach it either. This is a deep hole!"

"Charlie! Nellie! Nan!" Freddie shouted to the others. "Hurry up here!"

Nellie had wandered to the bottom of the hill, while Charlie and Nan were intently examining the ground beneath a clump of bushes on the far side. But at Freddie's call they all came running.

The little boy showed them the deep hole, saying his ball had disappeared into it.

"Say," Bert added, "maybe this is where the garnet went!"

One after the other the older children reached down into the hole, but not one of them could touch the bottom. And along the sides they could detect nothing but rocks.

"I have an idea," Charlie said. "Freddie, get me a medium-sized stone."

Freddie hunted around and came back with one. "Thanks," said Charlie as he drew some string from his pocket.

He looped the string several times around the stone and tied it. Then he stretched out on the ground and let the stone slowly down the hole.

He paid out the entire length of string but the stone still did not touch bottom!

"That didn't work," Charlie announced, sitting up again. "Boy, this hole is really deep! What can we do now?"

"We could try digging around it," Bert suggested. "If we made the hole larger, maybe we could look down it."

"Good idea! What can we dig with?" Charlie replied, looking around hopefully.

"There's nothing here," Bert remarked.

"Maybe Pickax would have a shovel," Nellie suggested.

"Of course!" Charlie agreed. "Let's go ask him."

The children trooped down the hill and over to the small house. The front door was closed.

"I guess he's not at home," Nan observed, after knocking twice.

"I'm afraid you're right," Bert agreed, "but let's walk around the house to be sure."

The children circled the little cottage, but there was no sign of Pickax.

"He must be at the mine. Let's go there," Charlie proposed.

The Forty-niners trekked over, but the shack was locked.

"There are a couple of shovels in the garage at home," Nan pointed out. "We could get those."

"Let's go, Charlie!" Bert started for his bicycle. "You and I can each carry one." The two boys hurried off.

The others sat down to wait. Nan and Nellie discussed Pickax's garnet.

"Wouldn't it be awful," said Nellie, "if the piece of ore did roll into that hole? We'll never find it then."

"I have a feeling we'll find it some place," Nan replied, pulling Flossie down beside her.

Freddie wandered around, looking for more woodchuck holes. In a few minutes the girls heard a faint cry. They looked up to see the little boy's legs waving wildly from under a bush.

"Help! I'm stuck!" he cried in a muffled voice.

Nan, Nellie, and Flossie ran to him. "Don't worry, Freddie," his twin cried, "we'll help you!"

Nan and Nellie each took one of Freddie's legs and pulled. The little boy slid out, a grin on his face.

"Why, Freddie Bobbsey, you imp!" Nan cried, "you weren't stuck at all!"

"I was just pretending to be a woodchuck," Freddie explained. "And I was a little bit stuck," he added sheepishly.

Half an hour later Bert and Charlie returned with the shovels. "We have a surprise for you," Bert called as he jumped off his bicycle.

"What is it?" Freddie and the girls chorused as they all ran toward the older boys.

"You guess."

From the basket on his bicycle Bert took a large black glass jar and a neatly wrapped package.

"What in the world are those?" Nan asked wonderingly.

"Dinah sent them." Bert grinned. "She was sure we'd get hungry and thirsty!"

While Bert and Charlie unloaded the shovels from their bicycles, the little twins eagerly took the packages.

Flossie tore the paper off quickly. "Oh! Coconut cake!" she exclaimed. "Yummy!"

"And ice cold lemonade!" Bert added.

The Forty-niners sat in a circle as he passed around paper cups of the tasty drink. When all the pieces of cake had been eaten and the lemonade finished the children started their work to enlarge the hole. First Bert and Charlie pushed the big stone away. Next the three boys, then Nellie, Nan, and Flossie took turns shoveling dirt.

Gradually the hole deepened and widened until it was about three feet down and the same distance across. Then Charlie, who had the shovel at the moment, called out:

"We've dug all the dirt away. This is an opening straight down through rock!"

"The entrance to a cave!" Bert cried out excitedly.

CHAPTER VIII

SKIN-DIVING SEARCH

WHEN Bert suggested that the hole might be the entrance to a cave, the children looked at one another in astonishment.

"How can we find out?" Nan asked excitedly.

Bert pondered the question. Then he snapped his fingers. "Charlie," he said, "suppose you lie down, take hold of my wrists, and lower me into the hole."

"Oh, no!" Nan objected. "That's much too dangerous! You might fall, and we haven't any idea how deep the hole is!"

"She's right, Bert," Charlie agreed. "We'll have to think of some other way."

Flossie spoke up. "Why don't we get Sam? He helped rescue Waggo from the mine!"

"Flossie, you're wonderful!" Nan exclaimed, hugging her little sister. "He's working at our house today, so we wouldn't be taking him away from the lumberyard!"

This time Nan and Nellie rode to the Bobbsey home. Sam had just finished his work and was glad to go with the girls to Mine Hill.

"This here rope's gettin' a good work-out!" he joked as he tossed it into the back of the truck next to Nan's and Nellie's bicycles while they climbed in front with him. "I have a good, strong flashlight, too."

When they reached the hillside Bert and Charlie each wanted to be the one to be lowered into the hole first.

"We'll make this fair and square," Sam said, pulling up two blades of grass. "The one that gets the long piece is the one who goes down the hole!"

The boys drew. Triumphantly, Charlie held up the longer blade of grass!

Sam handed Charlie the flashlight, then gently lowered him into the hole. The others all waited tensely until the rope slackened, showing that Charlie had reached the bottom.

Then they heard him call, "It *is* a cave! There's a pond here, and Freddie's ball is at the edge of the water!"

A few seconds later the rope jerked and Sam at the signal began pulling Charlie to the surface. When the boy reached the top he tossed the ball to Freddie.

"Did you see any sign of the ore with the garnet?" Nan asked.

"No. But it could have gone into the pond."

"How deep do you figure the water is, Charlie?" Bert asked.

"It looked pretty deep to me."

"Suppose I get my skin-diving gear and underwater flashlight and try to find the garnet," Bert proposed. "Sam, will you take me to get them?"

Sam agreed. The two hurried off and were back in a short time with the skin-diving equipment and a long ladder. Bert was wearing swimming trunks.

"We thought maybe the ladder would reach the floor of the cave, and you could all go down," he explained.

"Oh, goody!" Flossie exclaimed. "That will be fun."

Slowly Sam let the ladder down. The children stood around the hole, holding their breath. Then came a scraping sound. The ladder was resting on something solid!

"I'll go down first," Sam said. "Then if everything's all right, you can all follow."

A few minutes later he called up, "Okay, come on down!"

Bert went first, carrying his skin-diving equipment, then came Nan, Nellie, the little twins, and last of all Charlie. They stood at the foot of the ladder and looked around. The floor of the cave was smooth rock covered in places with sand. The top and sides were formed from huge rocks of various shapes and sizes.

"Ooh, it's bee-oo-ti-ful," Flossie exclaimed.

On the far side of the cave was a large pool of clear water. They walked over to it and looked down. The pool appeared to have no bottom.

"Well, here goes," Bert said, slipping off his shirt. He pulled flippers over his feet and adjusted his diving mask. Then he let himself down into the water, carrying the special flashlight.

Bert swam all around the pool, which he found had a rocky bottom, and was about ten feet deep, twenty feet long, and thirty feet across. The water was clear and very cold. In a few minutes he was up again. He took off his gear and quickly dried himself with a towel which Sam had brought along. "I couldn't see anything down there that looked like the ore with the garnet in it," he explained.

Nan looked up. "If that garnet did roll down the hole I suppose it could have landed almost anywhere in this cave."

While this conversation was going on, Freddie wandered off a little way. "What are those funny things?" he asked, pointing toward the ceiling of the cave.

It was covered with pendants, some of them the size of small pencils, while others looked like large clubs.

"Well, here goes," said Bert

"Those must be stalactites," Nan surmised. "We learned about them in school. They're formed by water dripping through the rocks and picking up minerals on the way."

"There are some stal-ac-tites sticking up," Flossie cried.

"I think those are called stalagmites," Nan explained. "They're really the opposite of stalactites. They're the result of the water dripping in one place on the floor of the cave."

"Thanks for the geology lesson, teacher," Charlie said teasingly.

By this time Bert was dry and had his shirt back on. Sam said he must get the truck back to the lumberyard, so they all mounted the ladder again. The good-natured colored man waved, got into the truck, and drove off.

"I have to go home," Nellie remarked. "I promised Mother I wouldn't stay out here very long."

"We all may as well leave," Bert agreed. "We can come back another day, maybe tomorrow, and explore the cave."

The six children walked over to the clump of trees where they had parked their bicycles.

"Look at this!" Charlie cried out, bending over his wheel.

"Of all the—!" Bert exclaimed.

"What's the matter?" Nan asked, running up.

Bert pointed to the bicycles. The back wheel

of each one had been securely tied to the frame with heavy cord. The wheels would not move.

"Bert, there's a printed note on yours," Nan remarked.

The piece of paper lay in Bert's bicycle basket, weighted down by a stone. Picking it up, the boy read:

"You Bobbseys think you're such good detectives. Let's see you solve this mystery! Ha! Ha!"

"It's not much of a mystery who did this," Nan said disgustedly. "Who else but Danny Rugg?"

The others agreed that Danny Rugg and Jack Westley had played the trick.

"Let's get the cord off fast. Maybe we can catch those guys and show 'em we solved the mystery!" Charlie proposed.

Bert grinned as he pulled out a pocketknife and began to saw through the heavy twine on Flossie's bicycle. This proved to be more difficult than he had expected as the cord was woven in and out of the spokes of the wheel. Finally all of it fell away and Bert turned to free Freddie's.

Charlie went to work on Nan's bicycle, then on Nellie's. In a few minutes he had them released. The two boys released their own, and before long the Forty-niners were pedaling toward town. Bert and Charlie rode fast, but they did not catch a glimpse of Danny nor Jack.

Charlie and Nellie went on to their homes

after waving good-by to the Bobbseys. The twins ran into the house, eager to tell their mother about the discovery of the cave.

Dinah called to them from the kitchen. "Mrs. Bobbsey isn't home yet. Bert, will you do an errand for me?"

"Sure, Dinah. What do you want?"

"Ride down to the store and get me a loaf of whole wheat bread."

"Okay." Bert started for the door. "Oh, Nan," he called. "Don't tell Mother about the cave until I get back, will you?"

Nan and the small twins agreed to keep the story for Bert's return. The Bobbsey boy hurried to the store and was just coming out with the bread when he saw Danny Rugg ride by on his bicycle.

Bert dashed out, calling Danny's name. But the bully pretended not to hear and rode on faster.

"Stop, Danny!" Bert yelled. "I want to talk to you!"

Danny paid no attention and turned the corner toward his home. Bert pedaled faster. But as he rounded the corner he saw Danny jump off his bicycle and run into his house through the front door. Quickly Bert parked his wheel and rang the Ruggs' doorbell.

Mrs. Rugg came to answer it. "Danny says he

doesn't want to see you, Bert," she said. "Have you two boys been quarreling again?"

"I just want to ask Danny about something," Bert replied.

"He has to get ready for supper now," Mrs. Rugg explained. "Come back and see him later."

"All right, Mrs. Rugg." Bert turned away.

As he went down the walk, he looked back. At a front window stood Danny making a face at him! Bert doubled up his fist as a sign he was ready for a fight, then went home.

At the Bobbsey supper table that evening, all the conversation was about the mysterious cave.

"I have never heard of a cave in this neighborhood," Mr. Bobbsey told the twins. "You children have really made quite a discovery."

"And Daddy, there are things called stalagmites and tites," Flossie said breathlessly.

Mr. Bobbsey laughed. "Well, my little fat fairy," he said, "you're learning things too!" This was Mr. Bobbsey's pet name for Flossie. "Sam tells me, Bert," his father continued, "that you went in the pool but that you couldn't find Pickax's garnet."

"That's right," Bert replied. "We're going to explore the cave again. The piece of ore with the garnet might have landed in some other part."

At this moment the front doorbell rang. Dinah

came from the kitchen to answer it. They could hear her open the door, then silence.

"Who is it, Dinah?" Flossie called curiously.

"Ain't nobody here," Dinah answered. "But someone sure rang that bell! Wait a minute—here's somethin' on the doorstep!"

A second later she came into the dining room holding a folded piece of white paper in her hand. "It says on the front of it, *The Bobbsey Twins.*"

Bert held out his hand and the cook gave him the paper. Quickly he opened it, then flushed as he read the printed message.

"What does it say?" Nan asked impatiently.

"Stay away from that hillside! No trespassing! The garnet is not there!" Bert read indignantly. "Some more of Danny Rugg's jokes. Can't he do anything but write notes?"

"Let's see it," Nan asked. After reading the note, she looked puzzled. "Bert," she said, "I don't think Danny wrote this!"

"What!"

The others looked startled and worried. Nan went to the hall and returned with the message which had been left in Bert's bicycle basket that afternoon.

"I'm sure these weren't printed by the same person!" she insisted. "This note didn't come from Danny—or Jack Westley, either!"

CHAPTER IX

MYSTERIOUS NOTES

"NOT written by Danny or Jack?" Bert repeated. "What makes you think so?"

Nan carried the two notes to the supper table and put them down side by side. The others rose to look over her shoulder.

"Well, in the first place," she explained, "the capital B in Bobbsey is made differently. One starts with a loop and the other with a straight line."

"You're right, Nan!" her father exclaimed. "You were clever to notice that."

Nan now pointed to the t's and g's in the two messages. "These are different too," she remarked.

"I'll have to hand it to you, Sis," Bert said a bit sheepishly. "You're a better detective than I am!"

Nan laughed. "I'm sure you would have noticed the difference too, if you had looked at the second note more carefully." She explained that she had seen some printing of Jack's in school and it did not look like that in either of the notes.

"Who could have left such a message?" Mrs. Bobbsey asked. "It worries me. I don't want you children to run into any trouble out at Mine Hill."

"Let's take the note to Pickax in the morning," Bert proposed. "Maybe he can tell us who wrote it."

"You and Freddie take it," Nan suggested. "Mother says that Mrs. Cottrell telephoned and invited us to come to the Rock Shop tomorrow. She is going to show us how to make jewelry. Flossie and I will go."

"I'd rather see Pickax than make jewelry," Freddie agreed cheerfully.

After breakfast the following day, the Bobbsey twins went their different ways, Bert and Freddie to the old miner's home, and Nan and Flossie to the Cottrells' shop.

Mrs. Cottrell first showed the girls the collection of rocks and minerals and explained where each one had come from.

"What's this kind?" Flossie asked as a rock of a beautiful shade of blue caught her eye.

"That's called azurite," Mrs. Cottrell replied. "It comes from the state of Arizona."

Then she picked up a piece of sparkling, greenish rock. "This is pyrite. It is found in many places, but this particular bit came from Vermont. It is called 'fools' gold' because it is often mistaken for real gold."

"I like this one," Nan said, picking up a bit of polished brownish stone.

"That's petrified wood from our far West," the shop owner explained.

"Can you always tell what each piece of mineral is?" Nan asked. "Some of them look a lot alike."

"There are definite ways to identify minerals," Mrs. Cottrell answered. "The easiest ways are by luster, streak, and cleavage."

In reply to the Bobbseys' questions, she explained that when crushed, a metallic mineral yielded a powder which is dark in color. "A nonmetallic mineral forms a light or whitish powder," she said.

"Do you always have to break up a piece of mineral to tell what kind it is?" asked Nan.

"No. You can give it the streak test."

Mrs. Cottrell told them that the mineral could be rubbed against a piece of unglazed porcelain. If it had a metallic luster, it would make a black streak. A white streak would mean the mineral had a non-metallic luster.

"And what's cleavage?" Flossie wanted to know.

"Cleavage is the word geologists use to describe the way a mineral breaks. If it breaks along smooth surfaces it is said to have good cleavage," Mrs. Cottrell explained.

"Thank you for teaching us about minerals," Nan said. "May we see how you make your jewelry?"

Mrs. Cottrell laughed. "Yes. I'm sure you girls have had enough lecturing for one day! I'll show you how we cut and polish a stone."

From a tray of stones of various shapes and sizes she picked up a three-cornered piece of streaked brown. "This is petrified wood," she said.

She held the piece by a pair of pincers over a small flame. Then taking up a metal stick about six inches long, she smeared the end of it with soft sealing wax. Next she pressed the stone into the wax and handed the stick to Nan.

"Now, this is what we call a dop stick," Mrs. Cottrell said. "Hold the stone against this revolving wheel. Just keep turning the stick to grind the piece into any shape you wish."

Gingerly, Nan took the dop stick and held the stone against the grinding wheel. "Oh, it feels funny!" she giggled. "I think I'll make an oval shape," she said, turning the stick slightly.

Mrs. Cottrell nodded. "That's right," she said. "You're doing nicely."

"May I have a turn?" Flossie asked hopefully.

"Just a minute," her sister replied. Then she cried, "Oh!" The stone flew off the stick and landed in the tray beneath it.

Nan's eyes filled with tears. "Have I ruined it?" she quavered.

"No. It was my fault," Mrs. Cottrell said comfortingly. "Do you remember when I held the stone in that little flame?"

Nan and Flossie nodded.

"That was to take the moisture out. If a stone is not thoroughly dried out, it won't stick to the wax. I was in a hurry and didn't leave it in the flame long enough."

Nan sighed in relief.

Mrs. Cottrell held the stone in the flame again, then stuck it on the dop stick. "How would you like to try it now, Flossie?"

The little girl put out her hand eagerly. She held the stone against the wheel, then carefully turned it until it was an oval shape.

"That's fine," the shop owner praised her. "I'll finish it for you." She pressed the stone against two other revolving wheels until it was perfect in shape and brightly shining. "Now it's ready to be put into a setting. I'll give you a lesson in that some other day."

"Thank you so much," Nan said. "We have really enjoyed our morning."

"You must have a souvenir from the Rock Shop," Mrs. Cottrell said. She took two chains from the drawer. On the end of each one hung a polished stone.

"The amber one is for you, Nan," she said, giving the girl a chain with a brown stone. "And the blue one for you, Flossie, to match your eyes. It's turquoise!"

"It's bee-oo-ti-ful!" the little girl exclaimed.

Nan and Flossie thanked Mrs. Cottrell again. Then they went outside and mounted their bicycles to ride home. Reaching the house, they learned that Bert and Freddie had just arrived.

"What did you find out about the note?" Nan asked eagerly.

"Pickax didn't recognize the printing," Bert told her. "But guess what! He said that hillside belongs to him and that we may go there any time we want to!"

"Goody! I want to look for the garnet some more," Flossie declared.

Mrs. Bobbsey came into the room as Flossie was speaking. "I can't let you children look around that hill if there's any danger," she said in a worried tone.

"We'll be all right, Mommy," Freddie spoke up. "Pickax is always around, and he won't let anyone hurt us!"

"Well, we'll see what your father says," his mother replied.

When Mr. Bobbsey came home to lunch, the twins told him all they had learned that morning and asked permission for them to make the trip.

"What about the cave opening?" he asked.

"We covered it up," Bert told him. "And when we took Pickax up to see it, he said he'd fix it so nobody could get in."

Mr. Bobbsey looked at the twins' mother. "In that case I'm sure it will be perfectly safe for the children to go out to the hill, Mary, as long as they stay near Pickax's cottage," Mr. Bobbsey remarked.

"They could always call him if anything happened." Mrs. Bobbsey agreed.

Her husband turned to Bert and Freddie. "I thought maybe this afternoon you boys might like to come down to the lumberyard. I'm expecting the final shipment of special lumber for the mine today. How would you like to help me check it in?"

"Oh, yes," they both said. "And maybe we could go with Sam to deliver it."

Freddie and Bert liked to go to the lumberyard and often helped Mr. Bobbsey when a large shipment of lumber arrived by boat. So when lunch was over the boys went off with their father.

When they arrived at the lumberyard, the special shipment had not yet been received. Bert settled down in the office with a magazine on lumbering, while Freddie ran out into the yard to find Sam. Soon the little boy was busily climbing around on the piles of neatly stacked boards.

An hour or so later Mr. Bobbsey walked out into the yard. "Sam," he called, "hasn't that lumber come?"

Sam walked around the corner. "No, Mr. Bobbsey," he said. "No sign of that boat yet."

"That's queer," the lumberman said as he turned back toward his office. "The supplier promised it for this morning. I guess I'll have to call him."

Mr. Bobbsey put in the call and talked a few minutes to the supplier. Suddenly Bert looked up. His father's voice sounded different.

"What!" Mr. Bobbsey was saying. "You say the order was canceled? I don't understand that! I'll call you back."

Seeing Bert's startled look, Mr. Bobbsey said, "The manager just told me he received a phone message yesterday canceling the order for that lumber. I'll find out if anyone here called."

He walked out of the office but returned in a few minutes. "Nobody here canceled that order," he told Bert. "I wonder what's up?"

"It must have been someone who doesn't want us to fix up that mine," Bert guessed. "But what reason would he have?"

Mr. Bobbsey shook his head. "I don't know, but I want that lumber!"

He quickly called the supplier and ordered the shipment delivered the next day. Then he turned to his son. "You know, Bert," he said, "your remark has me worried. I think we'd better get out to the mine and make sure everything's all right."

"Sure, Dad," said Bert, jumping up. "I'll get Freddie."

A short time later the three Bobbseys were headed for the old mine. When they arrived, Pickax and his helper had stopped work, and the place was deserted.

"We'll look around a bit," Mr. Bobbsey said as he unlocked the shack and led the way down the stairs. As he went he examined the supports. All seemed secure and sound.

Reaching the bottom of the stairway, he inspected the station carefully. Everything was in order.

"Oh, look!" said Freddie. "There's the giraffe!"

At the top of the incline in one of the galleries an iron car stood on the tracks. One set of wheels was much smaller than the other.

Suddenly Bert put his finger to his lips. "Ssh!" he cautioned. "Did you hear that?"

The others stood still and listened intently. There was no sound. Freddie started to speak, but again Bert motioned him to be quiet. Then they all heard the noise. There was a muffled thump followed by a sound of scraping. Then silence again.

Freddie's blue eyes opened wide as saucers. "The ghosts that the miners heard!" he whispered.

CHAPTER X

THE RUNAWAY GIRAFFE

"DON'T be ridiculous, Freddie!" his father said sternly. "You know there's no such thing as a ghost!"

"Y-yes, Daddy," Freddie agreed doubtfully.

"What do you suppose caused the noise, Dad?" Bert asked, trying not to appear too concerned.

"I don't know. Let's wait a minute, and if we hear it again, we'll try to trace the sound. There may be someone else down here, perhaps one of the workmen."

The three of them stood in silence for several minutes, listening intently, but the noise was not repeated.

Then Mr. Bobbsey moved. "Well, evidently there's no one down here," he said.

"It might have been someone up in the shack," Bert suggested, "and he's gone away."

"Perhaps," his father replied. "I'll look around here a little more, then we'll go on home."

While he resumed his inspection of the station, Bert and Freddie wandered over to examine the giraffe.

"Will it be all right if Freddie and I climb in the car and look at it?" Bert called.

"Yes, but no funny business!" his father replied, walking over to the far side of the station.

Bert boosted Freddie up into the old car, then climbed in himself. The little boy ran up to the front of the vehicle.

"Whee! I'm a miner," he shouted, leaning over the front of the car to peer ahead into the gallery. As he did so, he fell against a lever.

The car began to move!

Bert, who had been looking around the back of the vehicle, ran forward. By this time the car had gathered speed and was rolling rapidly down the incline.

"Whoa!" Freddie shouted. "Stop the giraffe, Bert!"

At that moment the car reached the unlighted part of the gallery, and Freddie screamed. The sound reached Mr. Bobbsey, and he looked up from his inspection of the flooring in the station.

Seeing the car disappear into the dark gallery, he grabbed one of the electric lanterns from the wall and began to run pell mell down the corridor.

In the meantime Bert reached the spot where his little brother was clinging to the edge of the swiftly moving vehicle. "Don't worry, Freddie," he cried. "I'll stop it!"

But Bert himself was very worried. They might crash into a dead end before he could halt the ore car. He groped around in the darkness and finally located the brake lever. With a mighty tug he pulled it back. The car slowed to a halt.

"Whew! That was close!" Bert sounded shaky.

As the boys caught their breath, Mr. Bobbsey

raced up, swinging the lantern. "Are you all right?" he asked frantically.

"Yes, Daddy," Freddie answered in a small voice. "Bert is a hero! He stopped the runaway giraffe!"

"And just in time," said his father, seeing a wall of rock ahead. "Good work, son! You might have had a bad accident!"

The two boys climbed out of the car and stood beside their father.

"What shall we do about the giraffe?" Bert asked.

"Leave it here," Mr. Bobbsey replied. "Pickax will know how to get it back. I'll go ahead with the lantern, and you boys follow me."

Holding the light high, Mr. Bobbsey made his way up the dark incline, his sons following close behind.

While Bert and Freddie had been having their wild ride in the mine, Nan and Flossie were walking slowly up the hillside above them hunting for the garnet which Ben Mullin had lost. Mrs. Bobbsey had happened to phone the lumberyard and had learned where her husband and sons had gone. She had told the girls, who had hopped onto their bicycles and followed.

"I'm going to look at every rock on this hill to see if there's a garnet in it!" Flossie announced.

Nan laughed. "That will take you a long time."

The girls made their way cautiously, looking carefully to the right and left for any sign of the piece of ore with the garnet. Several times Flossie stopped and bent over to examine a stone or small rock. But she had no success.

As the sisters reached the top of the hill and paused to rest, they noticed a man coming up the other side. His head was down, as if he too were hunting for something.

"Who do you s'pose he is, Nan?" Flossie whispered uneasily.

"Probably someone taking a shortcut."

When the man drew nearer they saw that he was short, stocky, and bald. The Bobbsey girls stood still, waiting for him to speak.

"You kids," he called, motioning them away with his hand, "get off this hillside! You're trespassing!"

Flossie looked frightened and turned away, but Nan stood her ground.

"We're not trespassers," she said firmly. "This land belongs to a friend of ours. He told us we could come here any time we want to."

"I don't know anything about that," the man replied. "The hill is mine, and I tell you to get off!"

"Come on, Nan!" Flossie pleaded, tugging at her sister's hand.

But Nan paid no attention. "We're going to stay here," she insisted. "What is your name?"

"It's Henry Zimmer," he replied and added rudely, "and I'll show you who owns this land! I'll come back and prove it!" With that, he turned and walked rapidly down the hill the way he had come.

"Oh, Nan," Flossie breathed, "you're so brave! I was scared!"

"There's nothing to be afraid of," Nan said stoutly. "Pickax told us we could come here, and Mr. Zimmer can't make us leave!"

Just then she and Flossie heard a call from the foot of the hill. The girls looked down. Danny Rugg stood there, motioning to them wildly.

"What do you want?" Nan called.

"Come down! I have something to show you!" Danny shouted.

Nan shook her head. "If you have anything to show us, you come up here," Nan insisted. "We know your tricks!"

"This isn't a trick. You'll be sorry if you don't come!" Danny replied.

Nan and Flossie sat down and pretended to be looking for something in the grass. When the boy saw that the girls were not going to do as he asked, he ran up the hill toward them.

When he arrived, Danny planted himself in front of Nan and Flossie, his legs apart and his hands behind him. "Guess what I've found!" he cried.

"A turtle?" Flossie asked timidly.

"Naw!" Danny replied scornfully. "This is something terrific!"

"What is it, Danny?" Nan asked.

"A garnet mine!"

The two girls looked astonished, then doubtful. "You know you're telling a fib, Danny Rugg!" Flossie spoke up. "You haven't found any garnet mine!"

"Is that so? Well, what do you call these?" The boy took his hands from behind him and opened one clenched fist. There on his grimy palm were three small dark red stones!

The girls pressed closer, and Flossie put out her hand to take one of the stones. But Danny closed his fist again and backed away.

"If you're so sure they're garnets, why can't we see them?" Nan asked suspiciously.

"These are mine!" Danny stated defiantly. Then he seemed to reconsider. "But if you like," he added, "I'll show you where I got them. I heard you were looking for one."

"Let's go with him, Nan," Flossie suggested. "Maybe we could find one for the Rock Shop lady."

But Nan still hesitated. She knew Danny well and doubted that, if he had found any garnets, he would tell the Bobbseys about them. But Flossie's face was very pleading, and after all, they did want to find a garnet for Mrs. Cottrell.

"We-ell," said Nan finally, "where is it?"

The boy waved his arm in a wide circle. "Over there. Just follow me."

"All right. But you'd better not be playing a trick on us!"

Nan took Flossie's hand, and together they ran down the hill behind Danny. When they reached the bottom Danny turned toward the woods where they had held their picnic a few days before.

"It's on the other side of these woods," Danny called back over his shoulder as he ran ahead.

For the next ten minutes he led them among the trees, turning frequently until both girls were thoroughly confused.

Finally Nan stopped. "I don't believe there is any mine," she stated. "You're just trying to get us lost!"

Danny looked hurt. "Why, Nan," he said, "I'm sorry you don't believe me. We're almost there!"

Suddenly the woods came to an end. Ahead was a low hill. Danny ran over to a depression beside a large rock. He knelt down and motioned Nan and Flossie to come nearer.

"Look!" he exclaimed, pointing to a hollowed-out spot by the rock.

In the dirt lay three red stones!

Flossie squealed. "See, Nan! It *is* a garnet mine!"

"How did you—?" Nan turned to speak to

Danny. "Wh-where is he?" she asked in bewilderment.

Flossie pointed. Danny was running toward the woods. In a moment he had disappeared.

"Now why did he run away?" Nan reflected.

The Bobbsey girls looked around them. "Are we lost, Nan?" Flossie asked, her lip quivering.

Nan studied their surroundings, then looked relieved. "No. Danny led us around in the woods, but we're back just about where we started from!"

Flossie sighed in relief, then stooped and picked up the red stones. "Well," she said contentedly, "we have some garnets. And to think Danny gave them to us! He must have a million more!"

"Oh, Flossie," Nan said. "I don't think these are real garnets."

"Oh dear," her small sister murmured. "Let's ask the Rock House lady," she proposed.

"That's a good idea! Come on, I think our bikes are just beyond that big tree."

The girls found them, and soon were on their way to the shop. Mrs. Cottrell greeted them.

"Can you tell real garnets from make-believe ones?" Flossie asked anxiously.

"Why, yes."

Nan told her about Danny's "garnet mine."

The jewelry designer said kindly, "It will be easy to tell if you have real garnets. You see, garnets have a non-metallic luster, leave a white mark on the streak place, and do not show good cleavage."

Flossie clapped her hands. "And may we see if these little stones do all those things?" she asked.

"Indeed you may," Mrs. Cottrell replied. "We will try the streak test first. If the stone doesn't make a white scratch on the plate, we'll know it isn't a real garnet."

She picked up a square piece of porcelain in one hand and with the other held one of Danny's red stones.

"Now watch," she said as she firmly drew the stone across the plate.

CHAPTER XI

A RETURN TRICK

NAN and Flossie watched breathlessly as Mrs. Cottrell pressed the stone against the streak plate and made a long scratch. No white mark showed!

Flossie looked questioningly at the shop owner. "Then it isn't a garnet?" she asked in a woebegone voice.

Mrs. Cottrell shook her head. "I'm afraid not. I think your friend was playing a trick on you."

"He's no friend of ours!" Nan stated firmly. "We should have known he was fooling us."

"But where did he get the stones?" Flossie wailed.

Mrs. Cottrell examined the stones carefully. "It looks to me," she said finally, "as if he had pried them out of some very cheap jewelry."

"Danny would!" Nan cried.

The girls said good-by to the Rock Shop

owner and thanked her for helping them. When they reached home, the girls found Bert and Freddie there and heard the story of their wild ride in the mine. Nan and Flossie in turn told the boys about the "garnet mine."

After supper, Freddie took his little express wagon out to the sidewalk. "I'll pretend this is a giraffe," he told himself, "and practice putting on the brake."

Giving the wagon a push to get it started, he ran along beside it, then jumped in. When he decided he had gone far enough, he "put on the brake." This consisted of putting his foot on the ground to stop the wagon.

He had done this several times when Danny Rugg and Jack Westley came strolling along the sidewalk. "What are you doing, Freddie?" Jack asked.

"I'm practicing braking," the little boy replied proudly, stepping to the sidewalk.

"Let's see you brake this," Danny said rudely. He put out his foot and gave the wagon a shove. The little cart sped down the walk and smashed into a tree!

"Look what you've done, Danny Rugg!" Freddie cried tearfully. "You've broken my wagon!" He began to pound the bigger boy with his fists. Danny gave him a hard shove, and Freddie fell down.

"Why didn't you put on the brake?" Danny

asked scornfully. Then, laughing, he and Jack ran off down the street.

When Bert heard about Danny's latest mean trick, he clenched his fists and said, "He's gone far enough! We must get even with Danny some way. Let's call a meeting of the Forty-niners and make some plans!"

Nan agreed and quickly phoned Charlie and Nellie. They too thought the trickery had gone far enough without a comeback, and promised to be at the Bobbsey home the next morning to discuss what could be done about the bully.

When they arrived the following day, Charlie declared, "I'm with you! Something *must* be done about Danny!"

"What can we do?" Nellie asked.

"We might lure him down to Lake Metoka and push him in!" Charlie suggested.

"Oh, we wouldn't want to hurt him," Nan objected. "And besides, Danny can swim. He wouldn't mind going into the lake."

"We could give him some April Fool candy with cotton in it!" Flossie said, giggling.

"Or we could take his bicycle and hide it right in his garage," Freddie put in.

While all these suggestions were being made Bert had been silent. Now he spoke up. "I think I have a perfect idea!"

"What is it?" Nan asked.

The children sat in a circle on the grass, and Bert explained his plan. It was greeted with giggles and exclamations.

"Do you think he'll come?"

"Oh, that's great, Bert!"

"I can just see him!"

"Call him now!"

Bert went into the house and, as the others

gathered around to listen, he called the Rugg house. Danny answered the phone.

"Hello, Danny," Bert began. "You know we're helping fix up an old mine, and we thought maybe you'd like to see it."

"Oh, yes? This is a trick. No, thanks," said Danny.

"This is a real invite, Danny," Bert insisted. "You'd get a big thrill out of the place. It's neat down there."

Danny hesitated a moment, then said, "Okay. I'll meet you at the mine at two o'clock."

Bert put down the phone and turned to the others. "Danny bit! Hurrah!"

The children shook with laughter, then Bert said, "Come on! Let's get things ready!"

Sam was working at the Bobbsey house that day, so the children took him into their confidence.

Charlie ran home and quickly returned with an old record player. "And I found this record," he said, "that has weird bird calls on it."

"Great!" Bert agreed. Then, turning to the grinning Sam, he said, "You start it when we give you the signal."

Sam nodded agreement.

Nan went into the kitchen and brought out a pair of Dinah's rubber gloves. "Let's fasten them to a couple of sticks, and just before we leave we can fill them with ice cubes," she proposed.

Freddie and Flossie found two sticks, and a glove was tied to each one of them.

"There! I guess that's about all we can do now," Bert remarked.

Charlie and Nellie went home to lunch but promised to be back in plenty of time. When they returned, all the children climbed into the lumber truck, broad grins on their faces. Sam drove them to the mine and unlocked the shack for them.

"Where shall I put the record player?" Charlie asked as they all hurried down the steps into the station.

Bert looked around. He saw several boards propped up against the far wall. "Let's put it behind those," he suggested. "You can reach it there, can't you, Sam?"

Sam nodded with a big grin. "I sure can, Bert. You just give me that signal, and I'll start her up!"

"Did you fix the gloves, Nan?" Nellie asked.

In reply Nan held up the rubber gloves. They were coated with moisture and a few drops of water had gathered on each fingertip.

Nellie shuddered. "Ooh, they look creepy!"

Bert and Nan turned to Freddie and Flossie. "We'll show you where you're to stand," Bert said. "You won't be frightened, will you?"

"Oh, no!" said Freddie stoutly, and Flossie shook her head violently.

The small twins were led down the gallery into the section where the light from the electric lanterns did not reach. There, on either side of the passage, was a small niche.

"You stand in one, Freddie," Bert directed, "and Flossie, you get in the other. When we bring Danny down here, you know what to do!"

They giggled and nodded.

Bert and Nan ran back to where Charlie and Nellie were waiting. When the four children reached the top of the steps again, Danny was just parking his bicycle.

"Hi, Danny!" Bert called. "Ready for an inspection of our mine?"

"I'm ready, but I think it's a silly idea," the bully answered.

Charlie winked at Bert behind Danny's back. "You know, the mine's supposed to be haunted. Maybe you can find the ghost!"

"You kids are a bunch of sissies!" Danny jeered. "You can't scare me with a lot of stories about ghosts!"

"Okay," Bert replied. "The tour starts here. This is where the old elevator used to be. Come on down these stairs."

The five children filed down the steps. Bert explained about the room at the foot which was called the station, then led Danny toward the gallery.

As they entered the corridor there came the shrill screech of a macaw. "What's that?" Danny asked nervously.

Bert looked surprised. "I didn't hear anything," he replied.

"Oh," said Danny in an offhand manner. "I just thought I heard a bird."

"You must be hearing things!" Bert scoffed. "There're no birds down here!"

At that moment an owl hooted. Bert and Charlie looked at each other. "I guess you're right, Danny," Charlie said. "I heard it too. I'm sort of scared. This mine may be haunted!"

"Haunted, my eye! You guys sure are scaredy cats!" Danny blustered.

"I wish I had your courage," Bert answered.

Danny looked at him suspiciously but said nothing.

By this time the three boys had reached the dark part of the gallery. "I—I don't think I'll go any farther," said Charlie, pretending to be frightened. "We might meet that ghost!"

"Well, I'm going on," the bully insisted. "I don't believe in ghosts, and you can't scare me!"

Danny pushed ahead of the other two boys. Soon he reached the part of the dark gallery where Freddie and Flossie were hidden. As he passed them they raised the sticks with the dangling gloves until the cold, clammy fingers just grazed Danny's cheeks! He stopped and then let out a shriek which echoed through the mine like an ear-splitting siren.

"Let me out o' here!" he screamed and dashed back through the corridor and up the stairs.

The Forty-niners stood helpless with laughter!

CHAPTER XII

THE INDIAN CAVE

WHEN Danny, pale as a ghost himself, dashed past Sam and up the steps of the mine shaft, Sam slapped his leg in glee. "And that boy says he's not scared!"

Bert stopped laughing just long enough to gasp, "He doesn't believe in ghosts!" Then he collapsed in mirth again.

Freddie was howling with laughter and dancing around. "I'm a spook, and Danny's afraid of me!" he shouted joyfully.

Finally all the children quieted down enough to agree that this time they had put one over on Danny Rugg.

"But how long will he leave us alone?" Nan asked.

Bert frowned. "Only until he finds out we played a trick on him," he said.

The next morning Nan proposed a trip to the cave at Mine Hill. "I think it would be fun to explore it," she said. "We really didn't look around much the other time. Will you take us, Mother?"

"Yes, I'd like to see the cave myself," Mrs. Bobbsey agreed. "But how will we get down into it? I'm afraid Dad needs that ladder you took before."

"How about my rope ladder that Daddy gave me for my tree house?" Freddie spoke up. "It's a nice long one!"

Mrs. Bobbsey nodded. "That's perfect."

Nan and Flossie went up to their room to get ready for the trip. Nan had on a fresh pair of blue denim shorts with matching shirt. She tucked a bright red handkerchief in her pocket and pulled a red sweater from the drawer.

"I think I'll wear a bracelet, too," she told Flossie, taking one from her little jewel box and snapping it around her wrist. It was made of squares of carved wood held together by elastic.

"Nan," said Flossie as she gazed at it, "I just love that bracelet! I'm going to wear my silver one." Flossie looked very cute in a yellow cotton playsuit.

When the girls came downstairs Mrs. Bobbsey was standing in the hall. "You look very nice," she said. "But Flossie, you'd better bring a sweater, too. You know it's always around fifty-five degrees in caves!"

Flossie hurried off for a yellow one, then Mrs.

Bobbsey drove off with them. Bert and Freddie had gone ahead on their bicycles with all the flashlights, including the underwater one.

When they reached Mine Hill she parked the car, and they walked up to the cave entrance. Bert and Freddie were there, rolling away the heavy stones that held down the boards over the opening. The others helped, straining and panting in their efforts. Finally the hole was revealed.

"We can fasten the rope ladder to this tree," Bert announced. "It's not far from the hole."

The rope was securely tied to the base of the tree, and the rungs of the ladder were let down into the hole. Nan tried out the ladder while her mother held her hand, and Bert remained at the tree to make certain that the ladder was holding solidly.

"It's fine," Nan announced, and started down.

At a signal that she had reached the floor of the cave, Flossie followed. Then came Mrs. Bobbsey, Freddie, and last of all Bert.

They all had flashlights which they snapped on, although a fair amount of light filtered down through the entrance hole. This time they inspected the walls of the cave more carefully. In one section the rock had been worn away in ripples which glistened in the light of the flash.

"Oh!" Nan caught her breath. "It looks like a frozen waterfall!"

"That kind of formation is called flowstone," Mrs. Bobbsey explained. "It was caused by water which poured over the rock many thousands of years ago."

"Look!" Flossie cried, pointing to a light brown rocky substance which hung from the cracks in the rocks. "It's just like taffy!"

"Taffy?" called Freddie, who had not been paying attention. "I want a piece!"

The others laughed, and Mrs. Bobbsey said he would hardly enjoy eating this kind of "candy."

"Here are two parrots!" Bert pointed out.

Pieces of rock had been worn away by the water in such a manner that they looked exactly like two birds perched on a branch facing each other.

Nan had wandered over to the underground pond. It covered one entire end of the cave. As she stood looking down into the water, an idea occurred to her.

"I wish we had a boat," she said. "Then we could examine the wall of the cave over there. Maybe the ore with the garnet in it bounced across the water."

"It would be fun," Bert agreed. "I'd like to explore over there, too, but I don't think we'd find the garnet. It's my guess that Henry Zimmer picked it up the day Mr. Mullin lost it."

Mrs. Bobbsey had been thoughtful. Now she spoke up. "Your father has an inflatable rubber boat at the lumberyard. Perhaps if you explained why you wanted it, he would let you bring the boat here."

"That's a keen idea, Mother!" Bert exclaimed. "Freddie and I will ride down there and ask him."

The boys hurried up the ladder and disappeared through the entrance hole. After they had gone, Mrs. Bobbsey and the two girls strolled around the cave. They saw many strange rock formations. Nan and Flossie took turns giving them names like *Monkey Eating a Banana* and *The Giant's Soda*.

Suddenly Flossie bent down and picked up something from the base of a large rock. "What's this?" she queried, holding out an irregularly shaped piece of stone. It was three-cornered with the outside edges ground to a sharp edge.

"Why, this looks like an ax head!" her mother exclaimed. "Flossie, I think you've found an Indian relic."

"Indian!" Flossie was startled. "You mean there are Indians around?"

Her mother laughed. "Not now. But several hundred years ago some must have been in here."

"Let's see if we can find any more relics!" Nan proposed.

The girls and their mother walked slowly around the cave, peering closely at the ground. Presently Nan spotted something. A broken piece of clay pottery, dull red in color.

Flossie rushed over. "Oh, it's lovely," she cried. "Maybe I can find a piece to match it."

The Bobbseys continued their search and in a short while had gathered a small pile of the broken pieces. "I believe these were part of a bowl," Mrs. Bobbsey said.

Nan declared she was going to start a collection of Indian relics. "These bits of pottery will be a good beginning," she said.

"I'll give you my ax head," Flossie said generously, handing it over.

Mrs. Bobbsey meanwhile had moved nearer the entrance hole. Suddenly she gasped.

"Why, girls," she exclaimed, "the ladder—" As she spoke Mrs. Bobbsey looked up, just in time to see the last of the rungs being pulled to the surface.

Nan and Flossie had jumped to their mother's side. They saw a man's bald head just disappearing from the top of the cave.

"Mr. Zimmer!" Nan cried out. "You let that ladder down again!"

There was no reply. Mrs. Bobbsey was furious. "What a dreadful thing to do!" she exclaimed and called loudly for Zimmer to lower the ladder again. He paid no attention.

"Oh, Mommy!" Flossie wailed. "Are we going to have to stay here forever?"

Mrs. Bobbsey assured her daughters that Bert and Freddie would be back soon and would be

able to help them. And after an anxious fifteen
minutes, Bert's head did appear in the opening.
"Are you still down there?" he called.

"Yes, Bert," Nan replied, "but Mr. Zimmer pulled up the ladder! See if you can find him!"

"And the ladder, too," Mrs. Bobbsey added.

Nan, Flossie, and their mother waited in silence for a few minutes, then Freddie called down, "Bert found the ladder hidden in some bushes. He's tying it to the tree. We didn't see Mr. Zimmer."

Bert dangled the ladder through the opening, and Freddie climbed down. Bert followed, carrying the collapsible boat. He said Sam had come along in the truck and was guarding the ladder.

"That's good," said Mrs. Bobbsey, who was still indignant at Zimmer's trick. "We might have been marooned down here for a long time before anyone found us!" she said.

"He probably ran away when he saw the truck coming," Bert guessed. "Zimmer's doing his best to keep us away from this hill!"

"Let's pump up the boat," Freddie said impatiently.

Bert had brought his bicycle pump, and in a few minutes the little rubber craft had been inflated.

"May I go out in it first?" Freddie asked, his blue eyes dancing with excitement.

"All right. Bert will give you a ride," his mother agreed. "Then Nan and Flossie will have their turn."

Bert set the little boat on the pond and held it while Freddie stepped in and sat down. Then the older boy got in and picked up a small paddle. "Now sit still," he advised his brother. "I don't want to have to fish you out of the water!"

Freddie giggled and settled down in the bow of the boat. Bert paddled slowly around the edge of the pond.

"Watch for the garnet on the other side," Nan called to them.

When the two boys reached the far side of the pond, they scanned the rocky walls carefully.

"Here's some more cave taffy," Freddie called, "but I don't see any garnets!"

When they had made the complete circle of the pond, they returned to where Mrs. Bobbsey and the girls were waiting.

"Let me take you next, Mother," Bert suggested.

When Mrs. Bobbsey had been around the lake, Bert got out and helped Nan and Flossie in. Their mother smiled. "It's up to you two girls to find that missing stone," she said.

"Okay, Nan, take it away!" Bert cried as he gave the craft a little push.

The boat rocked and Flossie squealed, but Nan grabbed the paddle and soon they were moving smoothly to the other side of the pond. When they had almost reached the wall of the cave, Nan gave an exclamation. "Oh, bother, the catch on my bracelet has come undone!"

She fastened it, but a few seconds later the bracelet fell into her lap again. "I'm afraid I'll lose it," she told Flossie. "I'd better take it back for Mother to keep."

When she reached the other side, Nan put down the paddle. "Mother," she called, "catch this!"

Mrs. Bobbsey held out her hands. Nan tossed the bracelet—but not far enough.

Splash! It fell into the water and disappeared!

CHAPTER XIII

THREATENING VOICES

NAN WAS aghast when her bracelet fell into the pond. "Oh!" she cried. "My beautiful bracelet! It's gone!"

Then suddenly Flossie saw the jewelry rise to the surface and float toward the center of the pond. "There it is!" She pointed. "What makes the bracelet float?"

"It's wood," Bert replied, as Nan quickly paddled over to the bracelet.

Before she could reach it, however, the jewelry was suddenly sucked down under the water. This time it did not rise again.

"Something's holding it down there!" Bert declared. "I'll try to get the bracelet."

Quickly he stripped off his slacks and T-shirt. Bert poised for a second on the side of the pond, then made a graceful dive, flashlight in hand. In a minute he came to the top, shook the water from his eyes, and said:

"Sorry. I couldn't find the bracelet any-where."

"Oh dear," said Nan. "Why was I so careless? I'll never see my pretty bracelet again!"

"I'm so sorry I couldn't catch it," her mother said.

Bert swam back and climbed out of the water. "Brr! It's cold! Wish I had a bath towel."

"We'll leave at once," Mrs. Bobbsey said. "The sun will warm you when we get up top."

As she had predicted, Bert quickly dried off and felt warm again in the sun. He put on his slacks and shirt, and they went home.

While the Bobbsey twins played in their back yard that afternoon, Nan could not get the loss of her bracelet out of her mind.

"Why did I wear it out there?" she sighed re-gretfully.

Bert was still trying to cheer her up when Charlie Mason came around the next afternoon. It was Sunday, and the Bobbseys had been to church and then eaten one of Dinah's special dinners.

Charlie had a twinkle in his eyes. "Nan, did you lose anything?" he asked.

"Yes, my lovely wooden bracelet!" she an-swered.

"I thought so," Charlie said.

"How did you know?" Nan asked.

"Well, it's quite a mystery," Charlie went on.

"Were you on the Lake Metoka beach when you lost it?"

"Charlie Mason!" Nan cried in exasperation. "What are you talking about?"

"Yes, Charlie," Bert spoke up. "What's the mystery?"

Charlie reached into his pocket and pulled out a bracelet. "Is this yours?"

Nan took it eagerly. The bracelet was battered and scratched, but the round gold disc engraved, *Nan Bobbsey,* was still dangling from it.

"Oh, Charlie! How wonderful!" Nan exclaimed. "Where did you find it? I lost it in the pond in our mystery cave."

"You did!" Charlie scratched his head in perplexity. "Then how did it get where I picked it up—out on Metoka Beach?"

Bert looked thoughtful. "You remember, Nan, how the bracelet was sucked down under the water. There must be an underground river running through that pond. Your bracelet was pulled down by the suction. The river current carried it out into Lake Metoka!"

"That's probably what happened," Charlie agreed.

"Then," Nan broke in, "perhaps the same thing happened to the piece of ore with the garnet. Maybe it's lying out on the beach this very minute!"

The children were excited at the idea and decided they would search the beach in the hope of finding Pickax's lost treasure.

Freddie and Flossie had been listening wide-eyed to the story of Nan's bracelet. Now Freddie spoke up. "Flossie and I want to go along," he insisted. "We're good searchers!"

"And I promised Mr. Pickax I'd find his garnet," Flossie added.

"Let's all of us Forty-niners ride out there," Nan proposed. "I'll call Nellie and ask her to come too."

In a short while the six children were pedaling toward Lake Metoka. Charlie was in the lead, with Nellie next to him.

"Tell me what happened," she begged.

"I was just walking along the beach," he explained, "looking for shells when I saw something shiny. I picked it up and there was Nan's bracelet!"

"It really sounds spooky," Nellie remarked. "Nan loses a bracelet in a cave, and it turns up on a beach!"

By this time the little group had reached the section of the shore where Charlie had made his discovery. They parked their bicycles against some trees and walked down to the sand.

They spread out in a long line and walked slowly up the beach, carefully peering at each stone. They saw no signs of the garnet.

Then Bert made a suggestion. "Let's wade along the shore. Perhaps we can find out where the underground river comes out."

"You mean because the water will be colder there?" Charlie asked.

"That's right."

The Forty-niners quickly pulled off their socks and sneakers.

"Ooh, the sand feels good!" Flossie cried, wriggling her toes.

The children were soon in the water and wading along parallel to the beach.

"I just stepped on something," Flossie called. "Maybe it's the garnet." Then she let out a shriek. "It bit me!"

Nan ran over to her little sister. "What is it, honey? Let's see!"

As Flossie lifted her foot from the water, a tiny crayfish let go of her toe.

Nan laughed. "He thought you looked good enough to eat!" she teased.

Flossie pouted a moment, then broke into a smile. "It doesn't hurt any more since he stopped biting," she announced.

Freddie suddenly cried, "I want to catch a fish!"

Bert looked at Charlie. "It would be fun to fish. I wish we had our tackle with us."

"We'll make some!" Charlie agreed. "What have we that we can use?"

The children waded to shore and sat down on the sand. Bert pulled a ball of twine from his pocket.

"This will do for a line," he said.

"I'll make a pole," Charlie offered and ran back to the clump of trees where the bicycles were. Quickly he cut a little branch from a sapling.

"And here's a hook." Nellie took a bobby pin from her blond hair.

"And I'll furnish the worm!" said Freddie. Running back to a grassy spot, he picked up a stone and began digging busily. In a minute he was back clutching a long worm.

Bert and Charlie crouched on the sand. They tied the string to one end of the branch. Then a stone was fastened to the end of the string.

"This is the sinker," Bert explained.

In the meantime Nan and Nellie had straightened out the bobby pin and shaped it into a hook. This was attached below the stone and Freddie put his worm on the hook.

"There you are, Freddie!" Charlie exclaimed. "Now for the fish!"

Eagerly Freddie put out his hand for the fishing pole. Then he walked down to the edge of the water and cast the weighted hook as far out into the lake as he could. The next minute the line grew taut and the pole bent.

"You have a bite, Freddie!" Bert cried. "Do you want me to take the pole?"

The little boy shook his head. "No, I'll bring in the fish," he said manfully.

"Boy! It's a big one!" Charlie shouted. "Look at it pull!"

The little boy struggled to bring in the fish, but each second he was drawn farther into the water. Suddenly he stumbled and sat down!

Bert and Charlie rushed forward and set Freddie on his feet. The little boy still held the pole, and in another minute had pulled in the fish.

"Look at that!" Bert exclaimed. "It's a bass!"

"It must weigh at least seven pounds," Charlie cried.

Freddie looked proud enough to burst. "I brought it in all by myself!" he boasted.

"You're wonderful!" Flossie threw her arms around her twin.

"Freddie, you'll have to get on some dry clothes," Nan said. "Why don't we all go home, and maybe Dinah will cook the fish for our supper."

"I was planning to have it stuffed and hang it on the wall," Freddie objected. Then he grinned. "But I guess I'd rather eat it!"

Later, when Dinah saw the big fish, she exclaimed, "My goodness, he's the finest bass I've seen in a long time. I'll fix old Mr. Fish right away."

Mrs. Bobbsey invited Charlie and Nellie to stay, and they telephoned their mothers for permission. When Mr. Bobbsey came home from a meeting at the church and saw the fish, he said:

"Well, Freddie, I guess I'll have to call you my little fisherman instead of my little fireman!"

Before the twins' guests said good night, the Forty-niners decided to go to see Pickax the next afternoon and check on the mine.

Freddie and Flossie were not able to go, as Teddy Blake was having a party for the younger children of the neighborhood. The older twins set off on their bicycles with Charlie and Nellie to call on the old miner.

As they neared the cottage where Pickax lived, the children noticed a dilapidated old car standing in front of it.

"I guess he has company," Nan observed. "Perhaps we should come back some other time."

"Let's hang around until whoever it is has gone," Charlie suggested. "We can sit over there under those trees and wait."

The others agreed. They parked their bicycles and threw themselves down under a tree a short distance from the house.

Bert pulled out his jackknife, and a lively game of mumblety-peg began. Suddenly there came the sound of loud talking from inside the house.

Bert glanced up. "Look!" he whispered. "That man in the window. He's the fake book salesman who ran away from Ben Mullin's house!"

"Are you sure?" Nan asked.

"Positive!" her brother replied. "He's tall and skinny and has the same mussed-up black hair!"

"What shall we do?" Nellie inquired nervously.

Just then they heard a loud, angry voice from the cottage. "You'll sign this paper or else—!"

Nan stood up. "I'm going in. Those men are threatening Pickax! They may hurt him!"

"I'll go with you," Nellie offered.

"Okay," Bert agreed. "Charlie and I will station ourselves by the car and be ready to grab anyone who comes out."

"But if you need us," Charlie put in, "just call and we'll come dashing!"

The boys walked toward the car while the girls made their way to the house.

At that moment the door flew open and two men ran out with Pickax following them. Seeing the children, the old miner cried out:

"Grab that paper! I didn't mean to sign it! They tricked me into it! I don't want to sell my mine!"

CHAPTER XIV

BERT'S DISGUISE

"I'LL get it!" Bert cried. He made a flying tackle at the man who was holding the bill of sale which Pickax had signed under threat.

At the same instant Charlie stuck out his foot and tripped the second man, who went down on his knees.

"Hold on, Bert! I'm coming!" Charlie called.

His chum was struggling with the other man, who held on tightly to the paper. But now, while Bert pinned the fellow's arms to his sides, Charlie grabbed the bill of sale from his hand.

"I have it," Charlie called triumphantly, and Bert released his prisoner.

"Why, that's Mr. Zimmer!" Nan exclaimed. "He's the one who tried to make Flossie and me leave Mine Hill!"

Zimmer's friend had struggled to his feet. He jumped into the car and called, "Come on, Henry! Let's get out of here!"

Zimmer lost no time in joining his friend, and the car sped away.

"So that's Zimmer," Bert said. "I guess we stopped him that time!"

The children turned and walked back toward the cottage. Pickax leaned against the door, trying to catch his breath. As Bert handed him the torn paper, he gasped, "Thank you, boys. Thank you so much. You've done me a great service!"

"What happened, Pickax?" Nan asked sympathetically.

The old miner told them that Henry Zimmer and his pal, Art Trask, had come for what they called a friendly visit.

Bert interrupted. "Is that tall man Art Trask? I've seen him before." He told Pickax about his encounter at Ben Mullin's house. "He's a fake book salesman, and he was carrying a garnet in a piece of ore."

Pickax looked surprised. "I'm sure Trask never sold a book in his life. He and Zimmer have always been miners, so far as I know. And as for the garnet, I don't think it's mine."

"I wonder," thought Bert.

"Why did the two men come to see you, Pickax?" Nan asked. "And why was Mr. Zimmer shouting at you?"

"He was trying to get me to sell my mine. When I told him I didn't want to, he threatened me."

"Then what did you do?" Bert questioned.

"I still said I wouldn't sell, and he started to leave. Then he came back and said would I sign a statement to that effect? Of course I said I would. He pulled this paper out of his pocket, and I signed it!"

"What is it?" Charlie asked.

"An agreement to sell! I didn't realize I had been tricked until after I had signed it. You kids came along at just the right moment!"

"Mr. Zimmer is mean and cruel," Nan declared. "He pulled up our rope ladder while Mother and Flossie and I were in the cave."

She also told the miner about the loss of her bracelet and how it had turned up on the shore of Lake Metoka. "We think perhaps the same thing may have happened to your piece of ore with the garnet, but we couldn't find it on the beach."

"It looks as if that garnet is gone," Pickax said, shaking his head mournfully. "I'll just try to forget it and make money on the mine. Are you children still going to help me fix it up?"

"We haven't forgotten," said Nan. "We're going to put some dummy figures of miners down there to show people how men looked and worked."

"That's right," said Bert.

Pickax got up and lifted an album from the table. "Maybe these pictures will help you. I took them when I was minin' out West."

The children gathered around to look at the book. "There's a good one!" Nellie cried.

Pickax examined the picture. "That's my special buddy, old Billy Grosh."

The photograph showed a man dressed in a pleated white shirt with the collar tucked in and the sleeves rolled up. He wore baggy denim trousers and a soft hat turned up on both sides. He had straggly chin whiskers which reached from ear to ear. Over his shoulder he carried a pick and a shovel.

"How many dummies shall we have?" Nan asked.

"Why not two?" Charlie suggested. "One with a pickax near the station and another one in the giraffe?"

"That's a good idea," Bert agreed. "But where will we get the clothes?"

"I can help you out there," Pickax offered. "I've got a trunk in the attic where I stored a lot of miner's duds. You can use them."

"That's wonderful!" Nan cried. "May we see them?"

"Sure thing! Come along."

Pickax led the way up the narrow stairs into his dusty attic. From under the eaves he pulled a battered old chest. When he lifted the lid the children saw a pile of shirts and trousers and several pairs of shabby boots. There were also four or five soft hats and some high, peaked caps.

"These are great!" Bert remarked. He picked up one of the soft hats and put it on. The hat came down around his ears.

"Oh, Bert! You look super!" Nan cried as the others laughed. "Put on the rest of the things!"

Her twin pulled on a pair of the baggy trousers, which were much too long for him. Giggling, Nan and Nellie found a belt and fastened the pants up under Bert's armpits.

Pickax joined in the fun. "If you'll go out to the shed in back," he said, "you'll find an old mine lantern. Then you'll look like a real old-time miner!"

Bert hurried down the stairs and out to the shed while the others selected clothes for the dummy figures.

A few minutes later, there was a knock on the front door. Pickax and the children went downstairs. When the miner opened the door, a woman stood there. She looked nervous.

"I'm sorry to bother you," she said, "but I was just passing your house, and I saw a crazy-looking old man going into your tool shed! I know you live alone, so I thought I should tell you."

Pickax was startled. "I don't know who it could be," he said in a worried tone.

"Oh, I hope he won't hurt Bert!" Nan cried.

"I'll go back there and see who he is," Charlie volunteered.

Just then the woman screamed and pointed. "There he is now!"

The others turned to look. Bert was just coming out of the tool shed!

"That's my brother!" Nan cried, doubling over with merriment. "He's not crazy!"

When the situation was explained to the woman, she joined in the laughter. "I see now he's just a boy, but from the back he certainly had me frightened!"

Bert apologized sheepishly, and the woman went on her way.

Swinging the lantern in his hand, Bert asked, "Is this the one you meant, Pickax?"

The miner said it was, then added, "Perhaps you'd like to use the caps with the lights on them, too."

"Oh, yes," Nan agreed. "They would be great!"

Pickax led the way to the attic again and from a trunk took two round metal hats. On the front of each was a small electric battery and a light bulb.

"When I was a miner out West in the old days," he explained, "we wore candles in our hats. But nowadays the lights are electric. We used these in my mine here."

"The hats with lights will be perfect for our miners," Nellie remarked. "What else shall we take?"

The children looked over the clothes again and decided on another pair of the baggy pants in addition to the ones Bert had worn, a striped shirt, a plaid one, and two pairs of boots.

"I think we have everything we need now," Nan decided. "We'll have a meeting of the Forty-niners to make the dummies."

"Would you like to walk up to the mine now,"

Pickax suggested, "and pick out the spots where you want to put the figures?"

The children nodded, and the little group climbed the hill toward the entrance to the old mine. When they reached the little shack and Pickax had unlocked it, Bert rang the bell.

"Just to let anyone know we're coming," he explained.

Pickax chuckled. "You'll be a miner yet, Bert!" he said.

The four children followed the elderly man down the steps into the station at the foot. They looked around admiringly.

"The work is almost finished, isn't it?" Nan queried.

Pickax nodded. "All we need now are your miner figures and some signs to explain what things are."

"That won't take long," Bert said. "And then you'll be ready for visitors."

"Yes!" agreed Nellie enthusiastically. "You'll make your fortune, Pickax!"

"I'll settle for less than that," Pickax said jovially. "I need just enough to buy my beans and bacon!"

Bert and Charlie had been walking around the little room discussing the best place to put the dummy miner.

"Would he be in the station, Pickax?" Bert asked.

"Why not at the foot of the steps?" the miner suggested.

"That would be great!" Charlie agreed. "The miner has just stepped out of the elevator-cage and is ready to go to work with his pickax!"

"And he would be the first person the visitors would see!" Nellie added.

"Now the other one," Pickax said, leading the way out of the station and into the entrance to the gallery. "Why not put him here?"

"He's the one we want in the giraffe," Nan reminded the miner.

"That's right. I can have the giraffe here at the beginning of the gallery where the light will strike him."

As he spoke he suddenly looked up at the ceiling. Then he shouted, "Run! Quick! Get out of here!"

CHAPTER XV

STOPEY AND GRIZZLY

THE FOUR children dashed back to the station just in time. A piece of shoring fell with a crash which echoed down the corridor! As they gained the shelter of the station, Nan looked back.

"Pickax!" she screamed, "he's hurt!"

By this time the dust had settled, and they could see the old miner stretched out on the floor of the gallery. A wood beam lay across his foot.

Quickly the children ran over to him. "If you can just lift that shoring off my foot," Pickax said, "I can get up." He was calm but had a pained look on his face.

Bert and Charlie bent over and pushed the beam aside. "Are you hurt badly?" they asked anxiously.

With the boys' help the miner struggled to his feet. He stretched his arms and stamped his feet. As he did this, he winced.

"My foot is bruised," he said, "but outside o' that, I'm still kickin'!"

"Oh, I'm so glad!" Nan exclaimed in relief.

"It's lucky all of us weren't hurt," Pickax said. "I don't understand how that shoring came loose!" He examined the beam carefully. "Looks like some o' the nails had been pulled out. Can't understand it!" He shook his head in bewilderment.

"Is the beam ruined?" Nellie asked anxiously.

"Oh, no!" Pickax reassured her. "We can put it back easy enough. No harm done!"

The children decided that their work in the mine was finished for the day, so they returned to Pickax's cottage to load the miner's trappings onto their bicycles.

"We'll try to make the figures tomorrow," Nan promised as they waved good-by to the old miner.

When the Bobbseys left Charlie and Nellie, Bert reminded them, "Next meeting of the Forty-niners in our yard at ten o'clock sharp tomorrow!"

The next day was bright and sunny. Sam set up the long picnic table under the big, old apple tree.

"There now," he said, grinning. "You all can get to work on those dummies!"

Charlie and Nellie arrived promptly. Then Freddie and Flossie came out of the house, each lugging a pile of old newspapers.

"This is for stuffing," Freddie announced as they dropped their loads onto the table.

"How shall we start, Nan?" Nellie asked as she helped Nan carry the miners' clothes from the house.

"Mother gave us two old pillowcases to use for their heads," Nan said. "Why don't we make the faces first?"

The girls spread the linen on the table and bent over it with crayons in their hands. Quickly Nan drew two circles with a line above each one. Then she put a dot in the center of each circle.

"Aren't those pretty eyes?" she asked with a giggle.

Nellie made a triangle with her crayon and then drew a line under it. "Nose and mouth!" she announced.

Freddie climbed up on the bench and gazed at the drawing. "It looks like a jack o' lantern," he said scornfully.

"I just had a thought," said Nan suddenly. "These pillowcases are going to make awfully white faces for the miners. Maybe Dinah would dip them in coffee for us so they'd look a little more real."

"That's a good idea, Nan," Bert agreed. "Give them to me and I'll ask her."

Dinah was glad to help, and soon the cases had been stained in coffee and hung on a line to dry.

"Let's stuff the trouser legs while we're waiting for the heads," Charlie suggested.

"All right." Nan handed several sheets of paper to Freddie and Flossie. "You two can crumple this up for stuffing."

As the little twins went to work, Bert and Charlie fastened shoes to the end of the trousers with thumbtacks. Then all the children began pushing the crumpled paper down into the legs of the baggy trousers.

At this moment Mrs. Bobbsey came into the yard to watch the process. She smiled at the bumpy appearance of the miners' "legs." "There is a barrel of wood shavings in the basement," she said. "Our new dishes came packed in it. Perhaps you could use that for some of the stuffing."

"Thanks, Mother," Bert said. "It would be better than paper, especially for the heads. Charlie and I will bring it up."

Nan, Nellie, and the little twins did such a good job of stuffing that when Charlie and Bert arrived with the barrel of wood shavings, the trousers were standing straight up alone!

"Boy, that looks weird!" Charlie exclaimed.

Just then Dinah came out of the house. She threw up her hands in pretended horror. "What happened to those poor men?" she exclaimed. "They've lost their tops."

Freddie and Flossie laughed delightedly at the joke. "They're hungry, Dinah. They've faded away 'cause they didn't have anything to eat!"

Plump Dinah chuckled. "I know somebody else that must be hungry. You just wait a minute!"

In a short time she reappeared carrying a large tray. On it were plates of ham and chicken sandwiches and a big bowl of potato chips. Mrs. Bobbsey followed with another tray holding cookies and a large pitcher of milk.

"Yum, yum, that looks good," said Freddie, climbing up on the bench and surveying the picnic lunch.

As the children ate the delicious food, they discussed the dummies. "They should have names," Nellie proposed, "so we can tell one from the other."

"Why not call one Stopey?" Bert suggested. "Remember Pickax told us a stope is where they take the ore out."

"And call one Grizzly!" Freddie shouted. "Grizzly can sit in the giraffe!"

"That's a wonderful idea, Freddie!" his twin cried.

After they had cleared the table and carried

the plates back to the kitchen, the children took the dry pillowcases down from the clothes line.

Nellie and Nan drew the faces on again. Then Freddie and Flossie filled them with wood shavings and tied a string around the bottom to keep the stuffing from leaking out.

"See!" Flossie held one up for Nan to admire.

Waggo, who had been sleeping under the tree, pricked up his ears. With a leap he was at Flossie's side. He snatched the pillowcase head from her hand and pranced across the yard shaking it violently from side to side.

"Waggo!" the little girl wailed. "Come back here!"

But Waggo was enjoying himself. Back and forth he raced with Freddie and Flossie after him until he suddenly dashed under a bush. There he lay panting, the pillowcase on the ground in front of him.

As the dog watched the small twins, his tongue hanging out, Bert crept up from the side. With a quick snatch he rescued the pillowcase head.

"Waggo! You're a naughty dog!" Flossie scolded.

Waggo's short tail pounded the ground. Then he put his head down and dropped off to sleep again.

Work resumed at the picnic table. Nan ran

into the house and returned with two pairs of her father's old gloves. "Mother says we may have these," she announced.

The gloves were pinned to the shirt cuffs. Then the shirts were filled with the crumpled paper and the heads attached to them.

"They look positively real!" Nellie exclaimed in admiration.

"Except that they're sort of wobbly!" Nan remarked doubtfully.

"I know what!" Bert exclaimed. He ran into the house and in a few minutes came back with an armful of wire coat-hangers.

"What are you going to do with those?" Nellie asked.

Bert handed two of the hangers to Charlie. "Straighten these out, will you?"

"I get it!" his friend said. "We can put these inside the figures to hold them up!"

"Good," Nan agreed. "We can fix the wire in Stopey so he will be bending over with his pickax!"

The four older children set to work straightening the hangers. The wire was stiff, and the job took a long while. Freddie and Flossie grew tired of watching and wandered off to play with Waggo and Snap.

"Come back, Freddie and Flossie," Nan called presently. "We're ready to wire the figures!"

The little twins ran back to the picnic table.

"I want to fix Grizzly!" Freddie pleaded. "He's my favorite!"

Nan gave the little boy one of the long pieces of wire, and he pushed it into the figure with the striped shirt through a hole in the neck.

"Now Grizzly can sit up straight," Freddie observed. "Shall I put wire in his legs?"

"Why not have him standing with his arms stretched out along the side of the car?" Nellie suggested.

"All right," Freddie agreed. "Then I'll put wires in his arms." He set to work busily.

Charlie and Bert picked up the figure in the plaid shirt. "I guess this is Stopey," Bert said. "Let's fix him now."

He got one of the long wires and began to force it down the dummy's back.

"Ow! You're killing me!"

The cracked voice seemed to issue from the pillow-case head! The children all looked startled until Nan noticed that Charlie's lips were moving.

"Charlie Mason! You did that!" she accused him.

Charlie grinned, then in the same high voice said, "It hurts to have wires in my back!"

The others laughed, and Bert retorted, "Now we're going to bend your back!"

When the wires had been inserted in the back and legs of the dummy, they were bent so that the figure appeared to be stooping. "That's perfect," Nan remarked. "We can put the pickax in his hands at the mine."

"Shall we take them out there tomorrow?" Charlie asked.

It was agreed that if Pickax could go with them the Forty-niners would set up the dummy figures the next day.

"We're getting closer and closer to our opening!" Flossie cried excitedly as Charlie and Nellie said good-by.

That evening at the supper table the twins

gave their father a complete account of their day's work.

"Grizzly and Stopey are bee-oo-ti-ful!" Flossie assured him. "You must come and see them."

A little later the twins led their parents out to the back yard. "We put the figures in the garage," Freddie explained.

With a flourish Bert opened the garage door. "There they are!" he announced.

Then he looked again. *Stopey was gone!*

CHAPTER XVI

STRANGE DIGGING

"WHERE is Stopey?" Flossie wailed as the Bobbsey family crowded into the garage and looked around.

Grizzly was propped up against the wall where Bert had left him, but there was no sign of the plaid-shirted Stopey. The twins looked at one another in bewilderment.

Then Bert spoke up. "I'll bet I know who's been here!" he said.

"Who?"

"Danny Rugg!"

"But how would he know about Grizzly and Stopey?" Nan asked in surprise.

"He and Jack are always snooping around. They probably came by here today and saw us working on the dummies."

"Danny is a mean boy to steal Stopey!" Freddie exclaimed. "I—I ought to go and fight him!"

Mrs. Bobbsey put an arm around her small son. "Now, Freddie, we don't know that Danny took your dummy," she said soothingly.

"Well, I'm going to find out!" Bert clenched his fists angrily. "I'll run over to Danny's house right now and ask him!"

At that moment Dinah came to the kitchen door and called to Mr. Bobbsey, "You're wanted on the telephone, sir," she said.

When the twins' father returned he had a worried look on his face. "I'll have to go out for a while, Mary," he told his wife.

"Is something the matter, Richard?" she asked. "Who was calling you?"

"It was the police."

"The police!"

"Yes. They said somebody just telephoned to report a man stretched out on top of one of the piles of lumber at the yard! I'll have to go down and see what has happened."

"Oh, Richard! I hope it's nothing serious. Do hurry along!"

"May Nan and I go with you, Dad?" Bert asked. "Perhaps we can help."

"All right. Jump in the car."

Mr. Bobbsey drove to the lumberyard as fast as he dared. Reaching the entrance, he jumped out. "Now stay behind me," he told the twins, "until I'm sure everything is safe."

Just then a patrol car drove up, and two

policemen joined the Bobbseys. They ran into the dark lumberyard, with the twins in the rear. Mr. Bobbsey went to a pole and switched on a flood light.

"We'll have to examine each stack," one of the officers said. "Stay back, children!"

Nan shivered a little. "Oh, Bert, I hope nothing terrible has happened," she whispered. "Why would a man be up on the lumber pile?"

"I don't know," her brother replied. "Maybe he was trying to steal some boards!"

The little group went on. At first they could see no one on top of any pile. Then suddenly, near the fence, they spotted a figure. Mr. Bobbsey scrambled up. In a moment he burst out laughing.

"Is this a friend of yours?" he asked, tossing a limp bundle down to the twins.

Stopey!

The two policemen grinned broadly. "A stuffed miner!" one said. "Now where did he come from?"

"He belongs to us, and he was stolen!" Nan declared.

The officers laughed. Mr. Bobbsey thanked them, and they went off.

"How in the world did Stopey get up on the lumber pile?" Nan asked in bewilderment.

"I suspect that your friend Danny had something to do with it," her father answered. "The officers said the person who telephoned sounded like a young boy."

"I'll get him for this!" Bert vowed.

Mr. Bobbsey shook his head. "If I were you, Bert, I'd ignore the whole thing. That will annoy Danny more than if you accuse him of the trick!"

"I guess you're right, Dad. We won't mention it to him. We'll just let him wonder!"

When Nan, Bert, and their father reached the Bobbsey home, Stopey was warmly welcomed by Freddie and Flossie. Mrs. Bobbsey heaved a sigh of relief.

"I'm glad it was only a dummy down at the yard!" she exclaimed. "I was worried."

"We'll put Stopey and Grizzly down in the mine tomorrow," Bert said. "Then they'll be safe from Danny. I don't think he'll go there again!"

The twins laughed, remembering Danny's flight from the "ghost"!

The next morning the Forty-niners set off for Pickax's cottage. Charlie carried Stopey on his handlebars while Grizzly dangled from the basket on Bert's bicycle.

When they reached the old miner's house, he was standing out in front. They parked their bicycles, then carried the stuffed figures over to him.

"I declare," he said admiringly, "I'd think

they were real if I didn't see their faces! Suppose we put these old miners where they'll feel at home."

He led the way up the slope, and they all went down the stairs into the mine.

"I think we decided to put Stopey right here." Charlie indicated a spot near the foot of the steps.

He arranged the figure in a bent-over position. Then Freddie clapped a soft hat on the dummy's head.

"Now you can't see his face, Pickax! Doesn't he look real?"

"He sure does, Freddie. And here's his pickax. Now he's ready to go to work!" The old miner laughed and slapped his leg.

"Let's do Mr. Grizzly next," Bert proposed.

The ore cart stood in the entrance to the gallery. Bert carried the dummy to the cart, tossed it in, then climbed up to arrange the figure.

"I think it would be funny to have him looking over the end of the giraffe, don't you?" Nan suggested.

Bert agreed, so the stuffed dummy was propped up at the end of the cart and his arms stretched along the sides.

"That's wonderful!" Nellie exclaimed. "He looks so real, it's creepy! I hope he won't run away with the giraffe!"

Pickax chuckled. "No chance of that any more. I've got chucks under the wheels so it can't move!" As he said this, he winked at Freddie.

The little boy looked embarrassed. "I didn't mean to start it the other day," he insisted. Then, to change the subject, he took the miner's hand. "Won't you show us where you found your big garnet, Pickax?"

"Okay. Come along." The elderly miner took one of the electric lanterns from the wall and started down the gallery. The Forty-niners followed.

On he went, past the lighted section, into the dark corridor. Suddenly he stopped and held up his hand.

"Do you hear something?" he asked.

Charlie answered, "Yes, it sounds like digging. Is someone down here?"

The miner looked uneasy. "There shouldn't be," he replied. "Let's go on a ways."

They walked along quietly, pausing occasionally to listen. The muffled sound of digging still reached their ears.

"It was right about here that I found—" Pickax stopped. "Why, there's been a cave-in! When did that happen?"

The children pushed up to where he stood. The entire corridor was completely blocked by big piles of crumbled earth and large rocks.

"I can't understand this," the miner said. "It wasn't here when we began to fix the mine up."

Bert was examining the fallen rocks. "It looks pretty recent to me," he commented. "The dirt is still loose."

He continued to poke around among the fallen rocks. When he reached the side of the gallery he stooped down.

"Look!" he cried. "This rock didn't fall here naturally. I think it was put here to cover something. Let's look!"

Pickax and Charlie ran over to him. "Together they tugged at the large rock. Suddenly it rolled away and revealed an opening ahead about two feet wide!

"I think I can crawl in there," Bert suggested. Kneeling on the ground, he squirmed through the opening.

"How is it on the other side?" Pickax called.

"It looks as if someone's been working here!" Bert reported.

"Stay there!" Pickax called. "We'll get some shovels and make this hole bigger."

He and Charlie hurried back to the station and got the tools. In a short time they had enlarged the opening enough for Pickax to crawl through. The children followed him.

Pickax stood up and swung his lantern around to examine the place. "It was in this part of the gallery that I found the garnet," he explained to the Forty-niners. Then he added, "You're right, Bert. It does look as if somebody's been in here."

"And we *heard* digging," Freddie insisted.

Flossie had wandered off to one side. Now she called out, "Is that your pickax, Pickax?"

"Where?"

The little girl pointed to the base of the wall. The miner walked over and picked up the tool.

"No, it isn't mine!" he said. "But see this!"

The children gathered around. Carved on the handle in crude letters were the initials, *H. Z.*

"Henry Zimmer!" Bert exclaimed.

CHAPTER XVII

AN EXCITING DISCOVERY

THE Bobbsey twins and their playmates looked at one another in astonishment. What was Henry Zimmer's pickax doing in the mine?

"How could Mr. Zimmer get in here?" Nan asked in a whisper.

"Do you suppose it was his digging that we heard?" Nellie wondered.

"How did he get away just now?" Charlie said in a low voice.

Pickax held up his hand. "One at a time, please!"

He looked around the chamber where they were standing. "I know every inch of this place, and I'm sure there's another way to get out of this section."

The old miner held his electric lantern high and flashed it around the walls. "Ah, there it is!" he cried. "That opening in the corner leads to another corridor which circles around and comes into this one back at the station."

Bert leaned forward and whispered, "Then if Zimmer was in here, he could have left by that exit when he heard us coming."

"That could be. But what was he doin' in here?" Pickax whispered back.

Nan's eyes sparkled. "Maybe we can trap him and make him tell us!" she suggested.

"A good idea! But how can we do it?" Charlie queried.

"Half of us go one way and half the other," she answered. "If Mr. Zimmer hasn't left the mine, he's probably hiding."

Pickax shook his head. "We can't try that. We have only one light."

"I have a suggestion," Bert whispered. "Why don't we make a lot of noise and pretend to leave? If Zimmer thinks we've gone, maybe he'll come back and we can catch him."

The others agreed to this plan. They hurried along the gallery by which they had come, talking and calling to one another. When they reached the station, Bert said in a loud voice:

"We ought to go home now, Pickax. We'll come out to see you again soon."

Pickax winked as he replied, "I should be gettin' home to fix my dinner, but I'll lock up here first."

They all clomped noisily up the steps. The old miner rattled the lock as if he were fastening it.

"Let's go back down," Bert urged in a low voice.

Nan had Freddie and Flossie by their hands. "You hide under the stairway," she directed.

The group began to creep silently down the stairway. When they reached the station, the little twins slipped into a space behind the steps.

Pickax, Charlie, Nellie, and the older twins flattened themselves against the wall next to the gallery entrance. They waited for several minutes, their hearts pounding.

Suddenly they heard a shuffling sound from the gallery, and a second later Zimmer and Trask stepped into the station. They were talking busily and did not notice the silent figures against the wall. Carefully Bert and Charlie slipped over to the gallery entrance to cut off any escape that way.

Pickax stepped forward. "All right, Henry," he said, "what are you two doing here?"

Zimmer, startled, stopped short. "Wh—why, we're just lookin' around."

Art Trask, after one look at Pickax, turned to run back into the gallery. Bert and Charlie blocked his way.

"Oh, no, you don't get away this time, Mr. Book Salesman!" Bert cried.

"I haven't done anything!" the tall, lanky man protested. "You can't blame me!"

"I can have you arrested for trespassing,

Henry," Pickax said to Zimmer. "You might just as well tell us what you're up to here."

"Well, if you got to know, we're lookin' for garnets!"

"Oh, so you did steal that garnet from Ben Mullin!" Pickax shouted.

"No, I didn't. I never saw that garnet!" Zimmer protested.

"Mr. Trask, you have it!" Bert cried. "I saw it."

"You never did! The one that rolled out of my pocket wasn't his."

"Prove it!" Bert cried.

Trask pulled a small piece of ore with a garnet in it from his pocket. Pickax looked at it. "That's not mine," he said.

Suddenly Trask turned on Zimmer and shouted, "You got us into this mess. Why didn't you steal the big garnet from Pickax when he first found it? Then we wouldn't have had to sneak in here and mine for others!"

"How long has this searching of yours been goin' on?" Pickax asked. "Did you two have something to do with the miners refusing to work here?"

Zimmer looked beaten. He confessed that when he heard that Pickax had found some ore with garnet in it, he had decided he would work the mine himself in the hope of finding more stones.

"I had to get you all out," he said, "so Art and me—we told the other miners that the place was haunted. We hid in the corridors and made spooky noises."

He smiled slyly. "We really had 'em scared! Then when you finally closed the mine, Art and me had the place to ourselves until these nosey kids opened it up again!"

"You mean you've been workin' down here ever since I closed the mine?" Pickax asked in surprise. "How did you get in? The shack was locked."

"We had a duplicate key. No one ever bothered us until that pesky dog fell down the shaft!"

Freddie and Flossie looked at each other delightedly. *Waggo had spoiled the plot to rob Pickax!*

"What was the idea of tryin' to make me sell the mine?" Pickax asked.

Zimmer replied, "When all this fixin'-up began, Art and me knew we'd be found out. So I figgered that if we could find enough garnets in here it would pay me to buy the place cheap. But you got stubborn!"

All this time Trask had been silent. But as Zimmer confessed more and more, the tall, thin man looked nervous. "I didn't have anything to do with that shoring fallin'," he protested. "Zimmer took those nails out!"

"I didn't mean to hurt anybody," Henry Zimmer whined. "I just wanted to scare you a little so you'd stay out o' here!"

Pickax looked stern. "You might have killed us! I'm goin' to turn you over to the police."

"Nellie and I can ride to town and get the police," Nan suggested eagerly, "while you and the boys guard the prisoners."

The old miner agreed to this, and the two girls set off on their bicycles. While they were gone Bert, Charlie, and Pickax continued to question the prisoners. Freddie and Flossie came from hiding.

"That cave-in was a phony, wasn't it?" Charlie asked. "You did it yourself."

"Yes," Zimmer admitted. "When you started to fix up that gallery where we were minin', we had to cut you off some way. We could always get out the other exit."

Freddie said, "You were the one who wrote us that note to stay away from our cave, weren't you?"

"And you pulled up the ladder so we had to stay down there until Bert rescued us!" Flossie accused him.

Zimmer appeared annoyed. "You kids are too smart for your own good!" he snarled.

Bert snapped his fingers. "The lumber order that was canceled. I'll bet you did it!"

"Art did that," Henry Zimmer confessed. "We wanted to slow you up in your work to give us more time to look for garnets."

"Why were you spying on us at Ben Mullin's house?" Bert asked Trask.

"We thought Ben had the garnet Pickax found, and I wanted to see if he was going to give it to you. You came out so fast I didn't have a chance to get away."

"Did you hear our conversation?"

"Yes," the man admitted. "I discovered that Ben had really lost the garnet. So Henry and I kept on workin' here tryin' to find some more stones. We tried first one corridor, then the other."

At this moment the bell in the shack above sounded and the group below heard footsteps descending the stairs. Nellie and Nan appeared, followed not only by two police officers but also by Mr. Bobbsey and Sam.

"Daddy!" Flossie squealed. "We caught the bad men!"

"Good for you!" her father said. "Nan and Nellie stopped at the lumberyard, so Sam and I came along to hear the whole story."

After the policemen led the prisoners away Charlie gave Mr. Bobbsey an account of Zimmer's attempt to take over the mine and search for garnets.

"I suppose he hoped to find enough of the stones to sell for industrial use as well as for gems," Mr. Bobbsey observed.

"Henry Zimmer was always tryin' to cheat somebody out of something," Pickax said. "I never did trust him."

As he spoke, they all heard the sound of shouts in the distance. They seemed to be coming from beyond the far wall of the corridor where Zimmer and Trask had once been working. The children looked at Pickax.

"What's that?" Bert asked the old miner. "More garnet hunters?"

Pickax looked puzzled, and they all went forward. "I don't know. I never mined that part of the mine myself."

"Ssh!" Nan cautioned. "Listen!"

The group stood in silence for a minute. Then they heard voices.

"Ho, ho!" came a shout. "The Bobbseys think we don't know about their old cave!"

"Danny Rugg!" Freddie whispered.

"They're in our cave!" Flossie cried excitedly.

Pickax's expression cleared. "I'll be hornswoggled! Zimmer and Trask must have dug almost through to the cave!"

"Let's scare the boys out of there and find out!" Bert whispered. "Sam, is that record player still here?"

"Yes, sir!" Sam grinned. "We'll just put those little birds on again!"

He got the machine and placed it against the wall next to the cave, then started the record.

"Whoo-oo," the owl hooted. Then, *"Awk-awk,"* came the macaw's reply.

At first there was no sound from the other side of the wall, then they heard a scrambling noise and Danny shouted, "I'm getting out of here!"

In a few minutes there was complete silence. Charlie grinned. "I guess that fixed Mr. Danny Rugg and his pal!"

Now Bert said, "Pickax, if our mystery cave is right on the other side of this wall, why don't we make an opening into it from here?"

"Why?" he asked.

Nan broke in. "I get it, Bert! That way we can have a double attraction for visitors—the mine and the cave."

"Sure thing!" Pickax agreed, his eyes shining in excitement. "We could even build another stairway and have two entrances and exits."

Flossie clapped her hands. "That would be fun!"

"We could take people riding in the boat!" Freddie suggested.

Mr. Bobbsey entered into the planning, saying it would not take long to put a stairway into the cave. "Pickax, you're almost ready to set up in business!" he exclaimed.

"Thanks to you Bobbseys," the old miner grinned.

Nellie had been quiet for some time. "Lots of mysteries are solved," she said. "But it's too bad we couldn't find the garnet for Mr. and Mrs. Cottrell," she observed sadly.

Nan agreed. "I still think it may be somewhere in the cave," she said. "I'd like to make another search there."

"Perhaps you're right, Nan," her father agreed.

Bert said excitedly, "As long as we're all here, I suggest we break through this wall right now and have a look!"

"Let's go!" Freddie exclaimed. "I'll get a pickax!"

CHAPTER XVIII

A REWARDING HUNT

"I HOPE we can find Pickax's lost garnet," Flossie remarked, "so the rock lady can make the earring for her daughter!"

The Forty-niners, together with Mr. Bobbsey, Pickax, and Sam, set to work with a will to break through the wall. Two pickaxes, two shovels, a sledge hammer and a crowbar were put to work.

The scene was lighted by the electric lanterns from the mine. First a small hole was made. Flossie and Freddie crawled through. Then a larger opening permitted the older children and the men to enter the cave. They placed the lanterns at intervals around the walls to make the search easier.

"Let's each take a section of the cave and search the ground and wall," Bert spoke up. "The piece of ore might have caught on one of the rock ledges."

"Ow!" Freddie cried out presently, as he bumped his head on a large stalactite. "A rock icicle hit me!"

When each section of the cave had been carefully searched, the group met again. No one had found the garnet!

"We've covered every place except the part on the other side of the pond," Nan observed.

"Let's take the boat over and explore," Bert suggested.

Quickly the little rubber boat was launched, with a lantern in the bow. It was decided that Mr. Bobbsey would take Flossie on the first trip. The little girl hopped in and crouched at the front. When she and her father reached the far side of the pond she held up the lantern.

"Shine it on those lower rocks of the wall, Flossie," he instructed.

As Flossie did this, a piece of rock above her head caught the light from the lantern. "Oh, Daddy, I see something!" the little girl cried out. "Pull a little closer!"

Mr. Bobbsey paddled over to where the rock wall met the water. On a ledge just level with Flossie's eyes when she stood up was a piece of ore with a large dark red stone in it!

"I've found it!" Flossie shrieked. "I've found Mr. Pickax's garnet!"

Carefully Mr. Bobbsey stood up in the little boat and lifted the piece of ore from its resting place. He handed it to Flossie and quickly pad-dled back to the rest of the group.

"Is this yours?" Flossie asked excitedly.

Pickax took the garnet from her and gazed at it. "This is mine all right!" he said, a little catch in his voice. "And I thought I'd never see it again! Oh, you blessed children!"

"Hurrah!" shouted Freddie, and the others gave whoops of joy that echoed back and forth in the cave.

"How do you suppose it got way over there?" Nellie asked in amazement as the excitement died down.

Bert answered. "It must have hit a rock on this side when it rolled down the hole and then cata-pulted clear across the pool and landed on the ledge!"

"I'm sure glad you children made us search in here again," Pickax said.

"This calls for a celebration," Mr. Bobbsey exclaimed. "I invite you all back to our house for a late victory lunch!"

"Oh, Daddy, that's fun," Flossie said as she hugged her father.

Pickax climbed into the car with Mr. Bobb-sey and Sam while the Forty-niners started off on their bicycles. When they arrived at the Bobbsey house they bubbled over telling Mrs. Bobbsey and Dinah about the great discovery. Then Mr. Bobbsey asked:

"Do you think you can feed this crowd of hungry sleuths?"

"Yes, sir, Mr. Bobbsey!" Dinah spoke up. "I sure can."

She was as good as her word. In a short while Mr. and Mrs. Bobbsey, the Forty-niners, and Pickax sat down at the picnic table in the yard. Dinah and Sam brought out bowls of chicken salad, hot biscuits, a tray of fresh fruit and homemade cookies.

"Dinah, this is a dee-licious vict'ry lunch," Freddie praised the jolly cook as he reached for another fluffy biscuit.

When everyone had finished, Nan suggested that Pickax take his garnet to the Rock Shop. "If it matches the one in the earring," she said, "I know Mrs. Cottrell would like to buy it."

"I'll be glad to sell the garnet to her," Pickax agreed. "But I think all the Forty-niners should come with me."

The children gladly agreed and set off with the old miner for the Rock Shop. Mrs. Cottrell was working at the polishing wheel when they walked in. She greeted them cordially.

"Mrs. Cottrell," Nan said excitedly, "we think we've found a garnet for your earring!"

"Oh, Nan, how wonderful! Do let me see it!" Then she called to her husband, who was working in the rear of the shop. "Albert! The Bobbseys think they have a garnet for us!"

Mr. Cottrell hurried into the room, and Nan introduced him and his wife to Pickax Pete. Then the miner pulled the piece of ore from his pocket and placed it on the counter.

"This looks perfect, but let's compare it with the other one," Amy Cottrell said excitedly.

She took the antique earring from a drawer under the counter. She and her husband bent over it. They measured the stone, then held Pickax's up to the light while the others watched intently.

Finally Albert Cottrell smiled at Pickax. "Well, sir, we'd like to buy this stone. It seems to be just what we've been searching for!"

"Yes," his wife agreed, "it's a true Lakeport garnet and just the right shade of red!"

Freddie and Flossie joined hands and danced around in glee. The older children all shook hands with Pickax.

The old miner smiled delightedly as he said, "I'll be mighty happy to sell it to you, Mr. and Mrs. Cottrell. I'm glad it's what you want!"

When the transaction had been completed, the Forty-niners said good-by to Pickax, promising to see him at the mine soon.

The next few days were busy ones. The twins went out to Mine Hill each morning to watch the progress of the work being done. A stairway and shelter were built at the cave opening. At

Mr. Bobbsey's suggestion a sign saying *Exit* was placed on the door.

"We don't want the visitors to get mixed up and try to enter this way," he explained.

"No," Bert agreed. "We're going to have a little table in the shack at the top of the mine shaft. Nan and Nellie will sit there and sell tickets."

One noon Mr. Bobbsey came home with important news. "The Lakeport authorities have inspected our work and have given Pickax permission to open the mine and cave to sightseers," he announced.

The twins cheered.

That afternoon the Forty-niners met around the picnic table in the Bobbseys' back yard to make posters announcing the opening. They cut large pieces of white cardboard and with black crayon lettered this message:

GRAND OPENING
SATURDAY
LAKEPORT MINE
AND
MYSTERY CAVE

"We can put the posters in store windows," Nan explained, "and on the town bulletin board."

"And we'll telephone everyone we know," Nellie added, "and ask them to come out to Mine Hill Saturday."

"We should have a real formal opening," Charlie said. "The kind they have for fairs and parks."

"Sure!" Bert agreed. "We can put a ribbon across the doorway to the mine shack!"

"And have someone cut it!" Nellie proposed.

But who? They all considered this problem, then Flossie said, "Why not Waggo? He was the one who found the mine in the first place!"

"Of course!" the others agreed.

The children put their heads together and with many shouts of laughter worked out a plan.

"Nan and Nellie have jobs—and Waggo—but what can the rest of the Forty-niners do?" Bert asked.

"You can be the head guide," Nellie suggested, "and explain all about the station and the gallery!"

"And the giraffe!" Freddie added.

"Okay," Bert agreed. "Then Charlie can take people out in the boat in the cave and show them where Flossie found Pickax's garnet."

"And where my bracelet went through the water tunnel to Metoka Beach," Nan said. "Maybe they'd like to try dropping things in and finding them later."

"That's a neat idea," said Bert. "It should bring lots of sightseers here."

"What can I do?" Freddie asked anxiously. "I'm a Forty-niner too!"

"Of course you are, Freddie," Nan said consolingly. "I know a very important thing for you to do."

"What?"

"You can put on your fireman's hat and stand at the foot of the stairway with your fire engine."

Freddie's face brightened. "All right! I really should be there in case of trouble," he said importantly.

Saturday morning was bright and sunny. The Forty-niners arrived at Mine Hill early to get ready for the opening. Pickax was already there dressed in his miner's clothes with the electric bulb shining on his cap.

He took the children on a last-minute inspection trip to make sure everything was in readiness. Then they came up and walked out of the shack. Bert and Charlie quickly fastened a white ribbon across the entrance.

By this time a large crowd had gathered on Mine Hill. Bert stepped out in front of the gathering and raised his hand.

"Ladies and gentlemen," he shouted, "You are about to see Lakeport's latest attraction, an old-time mine and a mystery cave! Mr. Waggo

Bobbsey, the discoverer of the mine, will now open it!"

Giggling, Flossie Bobbsey stepped forward, Waggo in her arms. Holding him up to the ribbon, she said softly, "There, Waggo!"

With his ears pricked up and his tail beating

the air, Waggo leaned forward and gobbled up the dog biscuit which held the ribbon! The mine and the mystery cave were open!

The crowd applauded and surged forward to

buy their tickets. The Forty-niners rushed to take their places. Flossie stood beside Freddie at the foot of the stairs.

"Don't be afraid of Stopey," she said to the first sightseers, two little girls. Flossie indicated the dummy figure with the pickax. "He's only a wood shavings miner!"

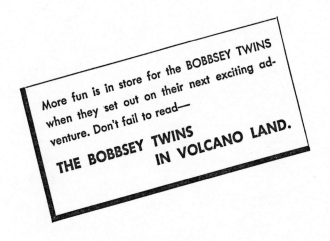

More fun is in store for the BOBBSEY TWINS when they set out on their next exciting adventure. Don't fail to read—

THE BOBBSEY TWINS IN VOLCANO LAND.